Dedicated to: Elaina, Matthew, and Sam

D1240624

Middle School Misfits:

The Stained Glass Tree

Leona Lugan

BOYS TOWN®
Press

Boys Town, Nebraska

Published by the Boys Town Press
13603 Flanagan Blvd., Boys Town, NE 68010

Boys Town Press is the publishing division of Boys Town, a national organization serving children and families.

Publisher's Cataloging-in-Publication Data

Names: Lugan, Leona, author. | Merriman, Kyle, illustrator.

Title: Middle school misfits : the stained glass tree / written by Leona Lugan ; illustrated by Kyle Merriman.

Other titles: Stained glass tree.

Description: Boys Town, NE : Boys Town Press, [2019] | Audience: grades 3-7. | Summary: With her country accent ... clothes that are far from cool … an odd, funny-to-pronounce family name (that earns her a terrible nickname) … Jilly feels like an outcast. Can she find a way to fit in while still being true to herself? Independent readers and middle school students will relate to the challenges and joys that Jilly and her schoolmates experience.--Publisher.

Identifiers: ISBN: 978-1-944882-35-8

Subjects: LCSH: Middle school students--Juvenile fiction. | Belonging (Social psychology)--Juvenile fiction. | Individual differences--Juvenile fiction. | Loneliness in children--Juvenile fiction. | Friendship--Juvenile fiction. | Self-esteem in children--Juvenile fiction. | Self-reliance in children--Juvenile fiction. | Social skills in children--Juvenile fiction. | Interpersonal relations in children--Juvenile fiction. | Children--Life skills guides--Juvenile fiction. | CYAC: Middle school students--Fiction. | Belonging (Social psychology)--Fiction. | Individual differences--Fiction. | Loneliness--Fiction. | Friendship--Fiction. | Self-esteem--Fiction. | Self-reliance--Fiction. | Social skills--Fiction. | Interpersonal relations--Fiction. | Conduct of life--Fiction. | BISAC: JUVENILE FICTION / Social Themes / Emotions & Feelings. | JUVENILE FICTION / Social Themes / Self-Esteem & Self-Reliance. | JUVENILE FICTION / Social Themes / Friendship. | JUVENILE NONFICTION / Social Topics / Emotions & Feelings. | JUVENILE NONFICTION / Social Topics / Self-Esteem & Self-Reliance. | SELF-HELP / Communication & Social Skills. | EDUCATION / Counseling / General.

Classification: LCC: PZ7.1.L8343 M537 2019 | DDC: [Fic]--dc23

10 9 8 7 6 5 4 3 2 1

Table of Contents

CHAPTER ONE
Rose is Turning Red

"Welcome to your new nightmare, Jillian. Please tell us what color underwear you have on today."

My new teacher might as well have asked that question on my first day at my new school. Don't teachers know how hard it is for new kids to stand up and talk in front of an entire room full of kids they don't even know?

"Jillian, we're waiting," Ms. Jenkins said again. "Please stand up and tell the class your full name, where you moved from, and a little something about yourself.

It wasn't the first sixth grade class I'd been to this year – and it probably wouldn't be the last, either. You would think I'd be good at introducing myself by now. Nope. I have been to at least 12 new schools since kindergarten. Every time I started a new school I had to get to know new kids, new teachers, and new rules. No matter how hard I tried, every school I went to, it seemed I didn't fit in. Oh well, here I go again.

"Hi – my name is, is Jillian – Jillian Lee Hicklenbilly. And I go by Jilly, by the way," I said to the room filled with brand new shoes – looking down at their feet made it easier to talk. I heard the kids giggle and whisper as I said my name. Of course.

"I moved here from Fair Play, well, actually, Humansville last," I said, which brought on even more snickers. "Those are *towns* in *Missouri,* by the way – that's where I'm from."

I needed to bring it to a quick close.

"And, I like to spend time outside, I guess," I said. "And, that's all."

"*Humansville*?" one of the boys asked. "Is that where they make *humans*?"

"No, it's not," I said nicely, trying to hide the aggravation I felt. "Is your town blue since it's named Blue Creek?"

"No, but the creek is," he said with a funny smile.

"Creeks aren't blue," I said, which made the boy look a little confused.

"Students, that's enough discussion," Ms. Jenkins said.

When I went to my desk, a girl said, sarcastically, "My name is – is – is… Jeely the Heeeelbilly," either because of my name, where I came from, or how I talked – all things that made me, *me*. I couldn't really change any of them. Ms. Jenkins, suspiciously, did not seem to hear her.

As I sat back down in the bright white school chair with its attached shiny, new desk, I heard another girl whisper, "Jillbilly the Hillbilly," behind my back, and of course, more giggles. Please don't let that stick, please, please, *pleeeeease*!

Oh well, I figured even if it did stick, I'd be outta here soon enough – probably over winter, or spring break, at the latest. You see, my mom didn't like to stay in one place very long since her divorce. I switched schools at least once or twice every year. That made me kind of an expert at new schools.

I got to know what each school had in common, like the fact most schools had five main types of kids: the athletes, the smart kids, the popular kids, the bullies, and the misfits. In my opinion, you could be more than one type of kid. Some of the smart kids were also popular, and some of the popular kids could be bullies, and on and on. The misfits, like me, were the kids who just didn't really fit in with any one group of kids at all.

"Thank you, Jillian, and welcome to Blue Creek Middle School," Ms. Jenkins said.

"Ms. Jenkins, I prefer Jilly," I said.

"Actually, Jillian, *I prefer* we use our given names in this classroom," Ms. Jenkins said, kind of stuck-up like.

Really!? I couldn't stand for that. I never went by my real name, *ever*! My name was the one thing that was *mine*, no matter where I was. This was not good.

"Oh, Ms. Jenkins?" I asked, in my most polite voice.

"Yes?" she said, just as polite as I did.

"Um, I have *never* gone by Jillian, so I would rather not start now if you don't mind," I said, with quite a lot of confidence. I added a nice smile to seal the deal. Whew, that was close.

"I do mind," she answered. "But the *good news* is you'll have a chance to become very comfortable hearing yourself called by your *given* name, *Jillian*."

She said it in such a way as to make it very clear there would be no more discussion on the topic. Some of the students giggled. Were they laughing at me? It was unacceptable. I had to act fast.

"Okay, *Rose*," I said, in exactly the same way she said my name. Her given name was Rose Jenkins – I knew it because it said so on the enrollment paperwork I filled out, which I always did for myself. My mom didn't like to mess with that kind of stuff.

Several kids burst into laughter, and Ms. Jenkins' face started to turn the color of her given name. First, it was a slight pink, then it worked its way up to medium pink, then her ears turned bright red, just like the pretty red roses we used to grow in our summer garden.

As her face turned even more red, the class laughed louder, except for one girl who was clearly unimpressed. As I attempted to stand my ground with my new homeroom teacher, the girl rolled her eyes so hard, and squished her face up so tight, I thought her eyes might actually pop out of her head. They didn't. That would have been bad if they did.

Ms. Jenkins' face got darker, and everyone laughed louder. The louder everyone got, the more I feared things were not going to end well for me. I was right.

"Enough!" Ms. Jenkins shouted to the class. Then she took a deep breath and very politely sent me to the principal.

THINK CRITICALLY...

- Have you ever been the new student at school, a new player on a sports team, or the new kid in a class such as painting, dance, or karate?
- Can you remember how it felt to be the "new kid" on the block?
- What are some things you could do or say to make someone else's first day better?

NOTES TO SELF:

CHAPTER TWO
Leprechauns Wear Green

My daddy, *may he rest in peace*, used to say everything you did had unintended consequences. He said they were the things that happened *after* you did somethin' if you didn't think real hard about what you were doin' *before* you did it.

He said everything had 'em, and the only way they could be avoided was to try to figure out what they might be before you said and did 'em. I can still hear him in my head, "If you do it right, you might be able to see the stupid in what yer' doin' before you actually do it."

I wished I'd remembered that conversation with my daddy before I called Ms. Jenkins by her first name, but I didn't. So I had to deal with a few unintended consequences. My first day at Blue Creek Middle School was not going as I hoped it would.

And by the way, creeks really aren't blue – most creeks I'd been in were muddy and dirty – some were clear, but they were *never blue*. What a dumb name for a school, and a town, for that matter.

The first unintended consequence was I got to meet the school principal, Mr. Michael, and not in a good way. He seemed very strict. Mr. Michael was a short, round fellow, with a beard, and a puffy face. He looked a lot like a leprechaun. In fact, it became hard to look at him without feeling the overwhelming need to giggle! He was even wearin' a green shirt!

He just kept talking and talking, about how disrespectful I'd been to Ms. Jenkins and that his school had expectations and stuff. I didn't really listen. I knew what I did was wrong. I could see the stupid in it as soon as the words slipped out of my mouth – but by then, it was too late. I thought about arguin' with him. I coulda' said I was just doin' what she said we were supposed to do – callin' each other by our given names. But, I knew better. I was just tryin' to get her to let me be in control of what I was called, like she got to be!

Of course, I also knew better than to admit that, so I just played dumb when Mr. Michael asked me to tell him why I did it. After all, I wasn't crazy! Now I had to write an apology letter to Rose – I mean "Ms. Jenkins" – before school tomorrow. Based on our first meeting, I don't think Mr. Michael cared too much for me. Hopefully, I wouldn't be seein' him ever again.

The second unintended consequence that happened was several of the boys fist-bumped me after class. Then, a couple of the girls said "hi" to me at lunch. I wasn't sure if me being rude to Ms. Jenkins was what brought that on, but my experience with sixth grade, and I was pretty experienced by now, told me it was. Kids in sixth grade seemed to like it when other students got in trouble. I have to admit, I liked that it took the attention off me and my name.

The third unintended consequence was I somehow made an enemy. Remember that girl who rolled her eyes at me like they were gonna' pop out of her head? It was her. She was the leader of some secret sixth grade club that still got away with bullying, even though my mom said we moved past that, as a society. Clearly, Blue Creek hadn't got the message yet!

Their leader, Brianna, pronounced, Bree-AHH-HH-nah, and I know, because she made it very clear to me at lunch. When she introduced herself, she took an extra, extra long time to pronounce the middle syllable in her name. She warned me to stay away from her and her friends. In my mind, I called them the look-alikes, because they all looked just like her from their pretty little heads and pointy noses, all the way down to their shiny new shoes.

As she walked away from me, she said, "You got that, *Jillbilly*?" and they all busted up laughing. Really!? REALLLY!?!? Why did that name have to stick? I knew I was stuck with it.

I couldn't even tell on her because sixth grade code doesn't allow for it. Everyone knows that. No one else tells, either. And where were the Bully Police in all of this anyways? Weren't they supposed to be out trolling school playgrounds, looking to take mean kids like Brianna down? Mom told me Blue Creek had a zero-tolerance policy for bullying so I did not have to worry about it here. But I knew better than to believe that. In my experience, that just meant kids hid it really good so they wouldn't get in trouble.

I decided I was gonna have to avoid Brianna,

and the look-alikes, for the rest of my life here at Blue Creek Middle School. That shouldn't be too hard, right?

THINK CRITICALLY...

- Why do you think Ms. Jenkins sent Jilly to the principal?
- Jilly thinks going to the principal was an unintended consequence of not thinking through a decision. What are examples of unintended consequences in real life?

NOTES TO SELF:

CHAPTER THREE
White Picket Fences

When I took the one-hour bus ride home that day, I decided to reflect on my day. My mom says we all need to reflect sometimes. She says the best thing to do when you reflect is to think about the things that happened in your day, and what you could have done differently to make them better. She used to reflect in the woods. She said it was the best place in the world for reflectin' and that you can usually always find the woods, no matter where you were.

The bus wasn't the ideal place to reflect, but at least I didn't have to worry about anyone trying to interrupt me – nobody even talked to me on the bus that first day. As usual, I was totally alone and I felt like a complete misfit.

While I was reflecting, I decided I would change back to my regular clothes tomorrow. On my first day, I wore shorts and a bright pink Nike T-shirt I got at the second-hand store. We couldn't afford that stuff, not brand new anyways. I don't know why I wore it in the first place. I guess I thought it would help me be more like them. It didn't work – even in my best clothes, I still didn't fit in.

Tomorrow, I was going back to my favorite pink camo shirt, my boot jeans – the ones that fit my ankles just right to make my boots look awesome – and my pink and brown cowgirl boots. They already thought I was a hillbilly, even though I tried to dress like them, so I might as well dress how I want. To tell the truth, I don't mind being a hillbilly, especially if it means livin' out in the woods and keepin' to myself, just like my daddy always did. I did not like nicknames that were meant to hurt someone's feelings, though.

I was so glad we didn't live in town this time. I've lived inside cities like Blue Creek before, and I didn't very much like them. I never seemed to fit in anywhere, but at home. My last two schools, back in Missouri, were pretty good, but they were made up of mostly country kids, like me, so fittin' in wasn't too hard. It was the movin' around all the time that made making friends difficult. I never even had a best friend, so my chances of ever being a *BFF* were slim!

I grew up in the country. Before my daddy died, *rest his soul*, my mom and me, and him, used to spend a lot of time in the woods. He even started to take me huntin' with him before he died. I think, if I needed to survive, I could hunt. The main thing is to be real quiet and still – no matter what! When I get older, I'm gonna' take up huntin' again.

Mom never liked to hunt. She thought it was violent, but daddy said it was about survival. She still liked being in the woods, though. Well, she used to, when daddy was alive. During the non-hunting season, Mom and I would go deep in the forest to pick mushrooms, berries, and to look for pretty rocks. She liked rock gardens. So did I.

My mom started getting sick after Daddy died, so

she made a place to rest on the couch. She got so sick she barely ever got up, at least when I was around. I started helping her out around the house because she just couldn't do it anymore. She didn't have anyone else but me.

Almost exactly a year after we sprinkled Daddy's ashes all around our woods, she introduced me to Steve. I didn't care too much for him, but I didn't mind him being around, either. Mom got a lot better after she met Steve. I wanted her to be well again, and happy. He moved into our house in the woods, but he didn't really like bein' out in the country. He made that very clear.

Steve didn't like cats. Who doesn't like cats? After he and Mom got married, they sold our house and bought a new house, closer to the city where Steve worked. I couldn't take my cat because he said it wasn't okay for outdoor cats to be in the city, plus, he was allergic. I had to give my cat to a shelter. They said she would get adopted, but she was old, and I knew what they did to old cats that nobody wanted anymore.

When I grow up, I'm gonna have my own animal shelter. People can bring me all their old cats and dogs and they can go inside, or outside, all they want! I won't hire anybody that's allergic.

It was hard movin' away from the house I was born in, but I figured it was probably best for Mom to get out of there – too many memories and all.

After we moved to the city, baby Kaylie came along and made everyone happy again. Soon after

Kaylie was born, Mom got sick *again*. Steve said Mom was just sad because she never really got over my daddy's death. That made him really mad.

I didn't know you were supposed to stop lovin' someone just because they died. He even said she wasn't really sick. He wouldn't help her with anything, not even Kaylie. Then one day, he just told her to leave. Me and Kaylie went with her. They got divorced.

It was just me, Mom, and Kaylie after Steve. We got along just fine without him. We moved a lot, but you get used to it, I guess. I wish we could've moved back to our house in the country, but it was somebody else's house by then.

Just as I was really getting into reflecting, the bus squealed to a stop on the dusty road. I had to get off and walk the rest of the way. As I opened the gate on the white picket fence that surrounded our house, I could smell something really good. Mom must have had the windows open because I could really smell it as I latched the gate on the old fence. When I got inside, there was a pot of stew bubbling over onto the burner. That explains why it smelled so good outside, but burnt stew water don't smell so good inside.

I turned off the stovetop and found Kaylie snuggled up next to Mom in the living room. She was watching some little kids show on TV. Mom must have fallen asleep again. The entire house smelled like burnt stew water – Gack! I grabbed Kaylie up in my arms from where she was snuggled up watching TV on the sofa. I accidentally woke Mom up in the process.

"How was your first day, honey?" Mom asked, through a long, drawn out yawn.

"Good – really good. How was your day?" I asked. Mom had enough troubles. She didn't need to hear me complaining about my new school.

"Your sister was a real handful, but we managed to make your favorite for dinner. There's a stew on the stove," she said, and then she snuggled back down under the covers.

"I know, it was boiling over when I got home," I said.

"I must have fallen asleep," Mom said. "I hope it's not ruined. Can you get Kaylie some stew? I'm not feeling too good right now."

"Sure. Do you want some, Mom?" I asked, hopeful she would have dinner at the table with me and Kaylie. She usually didn't.

"No thanks, sweetie. I'm just going to get a little more rest, okay? You know caring for your sister takes all my energy during the day, " she said.

"Yeah – um, I'll probably take Kaylie for a walk after we eat, okay? I kind of want to explore the forest," I said.

"Yeah, just be back before dark – and stay away from the river," Mom said.

"I will," I said, even though I had every intention of checking out the river – that was the best thing about being here!

"Come on, Kaylie," I said. Let's get some grub in your belly!"

"Okay, Jilly," Kaylie said, as she grabbed her favorite stuffed bunny. "Can Fluffy eat dinner with us?"

"Of course she can," I said.

"Fluffy's a boy, Jilly," she said, giggling. "You always get it wrong."

"Oops! Sorry, Fluffy," I said. "Now, be careful, Kaylie, the stew's hot. Make sure you blow on each spoonful 'til it cools down."

"Okay. I got to help Mommy with making your favorite dinner today. I even got to sprinkle the salt and pepper in the pot," Kaylie said.

"Aww, thanks, sis," I said. "You know you should only do stuff like that if Mom is with you, right? Promise me."

"I promise," Kaylie said.

"Good girl! Next year, you and I will be going to school at the same time so you won't have to be home alone during the day anymore," I said.

"But I'm not alone, Jilly, Momma's here with me!" she exclaimed, and then she rolled her big brown eyes and giggled. "*Silly Jilly!*"

"Right, I meant you won't be home at all during the day anymore," I explained. "I didn't mean to say alone. Just please be careful when I'm at school, okay, monkey?"

"Okay. Fluffy bunny thinks you're silly," Kaylie said.

"Thanks a lot, Fluffy! Okay, let me get my homework done so we can go explore," I said.

"Jilly, I miss our rock garden," Kaylie said. "Can

we start a new one? I was gonna make one for you today, but Momma wouldn't let me go outside by myself. I don't know why not. I'm not scared."

"We'll see, but she's right," I said. "You shouldn't go outside by yourself. Ever."

After I finished my apology letter to Ms. Jenkins and cleaned up the dinner mess, Kaylie and I headed out to explore. First, we followed the creek down quite a ways and found several deer paths in the woods. You could tell they were from deer because of the hoof prints in the mud. We also smelled a skunk nearby, but we didn't try to find it!

We found an old dump, filled with bottles and cans and other really old things. Most of the bottles were made of thick glass and were all sorts of colors, but mostly blue, green, and brown. Some were broken. I picked through the pile and set out the nice ones to bring back to the house. I'd have to come back to get them when I was alone because this stuff was too dangerous for little sisters.

While I dug through the bottles, Kaylie and I pretended we were diggin' for buried treasure. They sure were pretty when the sun poked through the leaves and hit 'em just right. I couldn't wait to get them home and cleaned up. Surely, I'd find some good use for the old bottles.

"Jilly, I found a pretty red one, but it's broken - can we fix it?" Kaylie asked.

"Be careful, Kaylie! And no, they can't be fixed," I said. "There's too much rusty metal and broken glass in here for you to dig around in. Come on, let's follow the creek down some more and see how far the river is!"

"But Momma said to stay away from the river," Kaylie said.

"I know what she said, and she said to stay away from it, which means we can still peek at it through the trees, right?" I said.

"I guess so," she said.

"But still, you prob'ly shouldn't tell her because then she'll get mad and we won't ever be allowed to explore out here again," I said. "You got it?"

"I got it!" she said.

And with that, we were off to do some real exploring!

THINK CRITICALLY...

- Jilly reflects on how her first day went while she rides the bus home. What are some things she reflects on?

- Do you think clothes and shoes are important to fitting in with particular groups at school, in certain sports, etc.?

- How would you describe Jilly's relationship with her younger sister, Kaylie?

- How is Jilly's family similar or different from yours?

NOTES TO SELF:

CHAPTER FOUR
Under the Silvery Moon

As we walked towards the river that day, against my mom's wishes, I was extra careful to make sure Kaylie was safe. I knew rivers could be very dangerous places – deadly even. We could hear the sounds of the rushing water getting louder. Kaylie was my responsibility and I didn't mind caring for her. It was really hard for my mom to take care of both of us, so I tried really hard to take care of me and Kaylie, to make it easier on her. My mom was kind of a misfit, too, I guess. She didn't really have any friends or anyone to help her out.

When we reached the sandy riverbank, I was amazed to see how big it was. It was the Missouri River. Since I moved to Blue Creek, Nebraska, from Missouri, I kinda felt like having the Missouri River close by was like havin' a piece of my home state with me. It was wide and swirly. It wasn't the kind of river you'd want to swim in, at least not here. A river that big could swallow a person right up if it wanted to.

We decided it would be okay to explore the riverbank, but not the actual river, that way I was still kind of obeying my mom. It wasn't long before Kaylie was picking up red and gray rocks that had been tumbled smooth by the big river. We always planted rock gardens wherever we lived. We used to have a vegetable garden, a flower garden, and rock gardens filled with all the pretty rocks we found. Now, because we move so much, we only planted rock gardens – that way, we didn't have to wait for them to grow.

As we walked along the riverbank pretending to be real explorers, Kaylie stuffed her pockets full of tiny pebbles. She was amazed at how smooth and shiny the rocks were as they rested on the sand. She found treasures, too, like a broken fishin' pole, three bobbers, and lots of big pieces of wood just layin' on the ground – some were full-grown trees! We had lots of fun climbing on them.

As the shadows started to grow long, I knew the sun was going to be setting soon and we should be getting back. There was only one problem. We were lost. I realized the deer path we took out of the woods looked like all the other deer paths coming out of the woods. I didn't want Kaylie to get scared, so I decided to make a game out of finding our way home.

"Let's pretend we're looking for a buried treasure and we need to look for clues to find it," I lied to her, but the last thing I needed was for her to get hysterical and start freaking out in the middle of the woods. "Now, do you remember seeing anything special or different on our way in, like a special tree, or a fence?"

"I saw a pretty rock for the rock garden," she said. "It was big. It would look really good right in the middle – it was in the creek we crossed to get here."

"You're a genius – give me five!" I said, as I lowered my hand for her to be able to high-five me. "We can look for the creek and then follow it back to the path. You'll make a fine explorer one day, Kaylie."

Soon, we found the creek and we were on our way home again. We didn't find the rock Kaylie thought she saw on our way in because it was starting to get dark, but I promised her we'd come back and find it. I also told her if she didn't cry about losing the rock, she could choose where to plant the rock garden. This made her run almost the entire way back to the house where we dumped our loot in the backyard.

"Should we put it over there?" I asked, pointing to a bare spot in the middle of the yard.

"Nope. I want it under that big tree, right there," she said, with her big eyes squinting in the setting sun. She was pointing to a large oak tree by the house. "That way, I can sit in the garden and be in the shade when it gets hot outside."

We set about planting our rock garden. When we were finished pulling weeds for the garden, we planted our first rocks in the dirt and made space for the new ones we would be adding soon. We got pretty dirty that day. I figured we better get inside to clean up. It was almost too dark to see by then.

When we went in the house, Mom was on the phone with someone. She was cryin' an' yellin' at whoever it was. It was usually Steve, Kaylie's dad. Then she started yelling at me for bringing Kaylie in while she was on the phone. I took Kaylie back outside and we played hide and seek until it was too dark and Kaylie was starting to get scared. When we went back in the house everything was quiet again and Mom was back on the couch. I could hear her crying, but I didn't dare ask why.

When Mom was especially tired in the evenings, or mad, I would take care of Kaylie for her. We would play games or find quiet places to sit and talk. Sometimes I would read to her. I tried to teach her things my daddy taught me, because her daddy wasn't around to teach her. I even taught her how to tie her own shoes when she was only three years old. It wasn't easy, but I was awful proud when I was done teachin' her. She liked when I taught her new things.

Mostly, she liked listening to me tell her made up stories about things at school, animals, and all sorts of things. Her favorites were the stories that didn't make any sense. It was fun telling her stories, and sometimes, I told her stories until I ran out of things to tell.

I gave Kaylie a bath that night and when it was finally dark, we went outside again. Ms. Jenkins said there would be a big, full moon that night, and I really wanted to see it. It was supposed to be extra bright. My daddy would have loved to see it!

When my daddy was still alive, we would go outside at night and stare up at the moon until I fell asleep. I was amazed at how much silver was in the sky. In fact, some nights the moon shone so bright it almost hurt my eyes to look at it, but Daddy assured me it wasn't like the sun. You could stare up at the moon and it would never hurt your eyes.

Some nights, there was almost no moon. That's when Daddy would tell me all about the stars in the sky. He knew all the constellations, and he even made up some new ones. He would show me where the planets were and tell me all about how the constellations got their names.

That night, as Kaylie and I sat on our blanket waiting for the moon to appear, the air was warm and breezy. As the big silvery moon appeared over the trees, I told Kaylie all about how the sun was actually making the moon look bright and that the moon didn't have any light at all. I don't know if she really understood what I meant, but she listened to every word I said.

Soon, Kaylie fell asleep and I was left sitting there under the big silvery moon all by myself. It was so bright I couldn't hardly see any stars! I carefully placed Kaylie's sleeping head on the blanket and closed my eyes. I pretended my daddy was sitting there with me telling me stories about the stars and the moon just like he used to do. Sometimes, I would pretend I was asleep just so he would carry me in. I really missed him. I wondered if that was why my mom was so sad all the time.

After the big silvery moon rose high up into the night sky, I carried my little sister in just like my daddy used to carry me in. I kissed her little forehead, went downstairs, and covered up my mom. I decided it would be a good time to catch up on my journal writing. My journal had a name – it was Sam. It stood for **S**imply **A**mazing **M**emories. When I wrote to Sam, I felt like I was talking to someone real. I told Sam things I didn't tell anyone else.

Dear Sam,

I have a lot to tell you today. I will start with the bad. On my first day at my new school, I met an evil beasty named Brianna. She was mean, but also really pretty, popular, and perfect. She's all the things I'm not. Her friends look and act just like her. They all sit together at lunch and laugh at everyone else. I also got a stupid nickname. Oh yeah, and I got in trouble AND no one sat with me at lunch. I wonder what kids like Brianna look like on the inside?

I think she might be all green and cruddy. If I was popular, I would be nice to the unpopular kids, and the new kids.

Now for the good... I went exploring with Kaylie and we found an ancient treasure, buried deep in the dirt. I saw something mysterious in the woods, but I'm not ready to talk about that yet. The moon was big and silver tonight and I took Kaylie to see it, just like daddy used to take me. I miss daddy.

I'll try to write again soon, but no promises.

Till next time,

Jilly

THINK CRITICALLY...

- Jilly really loved her father.
  How does Jilly keep her father's memory alive?

- Jilly does not have many adults in her life that she can talk to, so she writes in her journal, SAM. What does SAM stand for?

- Have you ever used a journal to remember things or process something that has happened?

- What are some things you could write about in a journal?

NOTES TO SELF:

CHAPTER FIVE
Bruises are Purple

Two weeks had passed since I came to Blue Creek Middle School before good stuff started to happen. Ms. Jenkins forgave me for calling her Rose and I was getting better at ignoring Brianna and the look-alikes. Oh, and I finally made a friend. I met Anton on the bus. He was a sixth-grader like me, but he was in Miss Manchester's homeroom, so we didn't see each other a lot at school.

Anton was nice (and cute). He just started talking to me on the way to school one morning, like we were always friends. Turns out, he lives just down the road from me, about a mile away, with his aunt and uncle. One day on the ride home from school, he asked if he could sit with me. I said yes. He was a good artist. He drew on everything – his notebooks, his arms, he even drew on his shoes! Each day on the bus, he worked on some kind of art. He was very talented.

"Why do you do that?" I asked him.

"Do what?" he asked.

"Draw on everything," I said.

"I don't know, because I like it, I guess," he said. "It makes me feel good."

"Can you make something for me?" I asked.

"Sure, what's your favorite color?" he said.

"Oh, I don't have just one favorite color," I said. "There are too many beautiful colors out there.

To choose just one wouldn't be fair to all the other colors."

"Well, what are your top three favorite colors?" he asked.

"I guess silver because it reminds me of the moon, and white because I like the white picket fence around my house – it makes me feel safe," I said. "Then there's red, like on the wing of a red-winged blackbird, and green for the trees in the forest, and yellow like the sun…"

"Okay, I get it, you like all the colors!" he said, laughing, as the big yellow bus rolled to a stop. We made our first official after-school plans for the next day. I couldn't wait!

The next day at school was really long. It must have been the longest day of my life. Every time I looked at the clock, it seemed to be moving at sloth-speed.

Finally, the bell rang! The wait was over. I was so excited to get on the bus I almost left my backpack in my locker. As I waited in the bus line, Anton came walking over to me.

"Hey, Jilly, are we still going to hang out after school today?" he asked, as the bus driver opened the old creaky bus doors. "My uncle said I have to be home by five o'clock."

"Yeah," I said, all cool-like, but I could feel my cheeks heating up. Knowing I was actually going to have a friend over was more than I could stand! As the bus dropped off each student, I told Anton all about the old dump. We were going to check it out first and then I might even show him the mysterious thing I found, if we had time.

When we got off the bus, he told me jokes as we walked the long pathway leading to the old white farmhouse I called home. I laughed so hard, tears came out of my eyeballs.

"Did you hear the one about the chicken who could fly?" he asked, as we finally made it into my yard.

But I didn't answer.

I could tell something was wrong as soon as we walked up. The front door was wide open and I didn't see Kaylie anywhere. Mom was sound asleep on the sofa. Kaylie was gone.

"Mom, Mom, get up – where's Kaylie?" I asked.

"What? She's right here. Stop shouting!" Mom said, as she pulled the covers up over her head.

"Mom – no – she's not!" I screamed. Mom tried to get up, but she couldn't. She mumbled something I couldn't hear and laid back down. Before I left the house to search the yard, Mom was back to sleep.

"Calm down, Jilly, she's got to be around here somewhere," Anton said. "Where does she like to play?"

"The rock garden!" I said. Yes, she had to be there. I went straight to the rock garden, but no Kaylie. The rocks in the rock garden were moved around so I knew she had been out there at some point.

"Anton, go look around the yard, please." I said. My stomach was jumping out of my gut. Anton ran around the entire house, but found no sign of Kaylie.

"I don't understand it. The rock garden is her favorite place. That's where she goes when she's scared," I said. My mind was racing a hundred miles a minute. I showed Anton how the rocks had been moved. Did something happen to her? Did someone take her?

"What about the woods?" Anton asked. "Would she wander off?"

"I don't think so," I said, but then I remembered the rock. "Wait – there's the river – a rock – it – it's down by river. Oh my goodness! She's down by the river looking for a rock!"

"The river!?" Anton asked, incredulously. "How old is she?"

"She's four. I'm really sorry, Anton, but I have to go find my sister," I said. "You – you better go home. I'm really sorry you came over, but I have to go."

"Na, na, na," he said, shaking his head back and forth. "That's not happening. You're my friend, Jilly, and I'm coming with you. I'm gonna help you find your little sister."

"You sure?" I asked, not wanting to burden my new friend, but really hoping he would help me.

"You got it," Anton said, and then he headed in the direction of the river. He began calling Kaylie's name. I had to run to catch up to him. Soon, we were almost all the way to the river, but there was no sign of Kaylie anywhere. My lungs were on fire from running and my heart pounded against my chest.

"Wait," Anton said. "I heard something – over there!" He pointed in the direction of a bluff. "Jilly, STOP – be quiet and see if we can hear it again," he urged.

"Okay – I need to catch my breath anyway," I said. I was becoming desperate to find her. "Kaylie! KAAY-LIEEE! Can you hear me? It's Jilly!" I thought I heard her crying in the distance, but the rushing water from the river was too loud.

"Let's split up – you head up top of the bluff. I'll stick to the riverside. We'll find her, Jilly," Anton said, as he grabbed my hand and squeezed it tight. "We'll find her. Let's go."

I climbed to the topside of the bluff as I continued to call for my little sister. I couldn't bear the thought of something bad happening to her. In my head, I started to go through all the terrible things that could have happened to her, but Anton screamed out to me, "I found her! She's alright. Get down here."

When I got to Kaylie, I noticed she had a big purple bruise on her arm and her face was scratched, but that was it. She was okay.

"Kaylie, what are you doing here, and by yourself?" I said.

"I'm sorry, Jilly, I was just looking for pretty rocks for the garden," she said, before starting to cry. "I'm sorry."

"It's okay, Kaylie-bug! I love you. I'm just glad you're okay!" I said.

"Are you gonna tell Momma, Jilly?" Kaylie asked.

"No, Momma's sick today, Kaylie. It's best if we don't tell her," I answered.

On our way back, I showed Anton the dump. The evening sun was hitting the old bottles just right so they sparkled in all their beautiful colors. The broken ones looked especially pretty in the evening sunlight. We took a minute to look at a couple of them.

"Well, lookie here," Anton said, handing a tiny purple bottle to Kaylie. "I think this one matches your bruise perfectly."

"It's pretty, can I have it?" Kaylie asked.

"Yes, ma'am," Anton said. "You better keep it; it's the prettiest bottle here – just like you, Kaylie."

"Thank you, Anton," Kaylie said, as she held tight to the pretty purple bottle with her chunky little fingers. "I will keep it forever."

Anton carried Kaylie all the way back to the house. He told her a few silly jokes to take her mind of off what happened.

"What's the difference between a green apple and a red apple?" Anton asked Kaylie.

"One's green and one's red," Kaylie answered.

"Nope, one's orange and one's blue," Anton said with a goofy look on his face.

"What? Nuh-uh," Kaylie said between giggles. "You're silly, Anton, and you're wrong!"

By the time we got back, it was almost time for Anton to go home, but we had a little while yet, so we walked around the yard and talked. He told me he had a hard time making friends because he felt out of place in Blue Creek. He said it was a lot different in Chicago. He had only been here for a year and it was hard fitting in. He said his mom had made some mistakes and he and his brothers had to live with his Aunt Lou and Uncle George.

"You know, Anton, it's hard being a country girl this close to the city. Everyone thinks I'm different just cause of the way I dress, and how I talk, so I understand," I told him.

"I know, Jilly, but I'm one of only a few black kids that go to school here and believe it or not, some people treat me differently just because of the color of my skin," Anton said. "My mom always taught me what matters is on the inside. Not everyone sees it that way, and I think that is something you and I have in common – people treat us differently because of what they think they know about us – not what's on the inside."

Soon, it was time for Anton to leave. I stayed outside for a while thinking about our conversation. I was happy to have found a friend who understood how I felt – we were different, but the same.

I think that day was one of the worst days of my life – and one of the best. I felt like I finally found a real friend in Anton. I couldn't believe he helped me find Kaylie – I can't even imagine what would have happened if he wasn't there with me that day. I figured it must have been fate that brought us together.

THINK CRITICALLY...

- How would have Jilly's day been different if Anton did not come home with her?
- What is happening with Jilly's mom?
- Who can Jilly call in an emergency?
- Who are some people in your life you can call in an emergency?

CHAPTER SIX
Piglets are Pink

"What's that?" I asked Anton, as I sat my tray down on the lunch table. He was drawing some kind of design. It was full of different colors, lines, and blocks. It was some sort of pattern.

"It's a picture," he said, with a smile.

"Well, duh, I know that, what's it of?" I asked him.

"Look closer, can you see a giraffe?" he asked.

"Oh my Gosh, that's awesome," I said, as I noticed the giraffe hidden among the zig-zagging lines. "Are you doing that for art class or something?"

"Na, na, na," he said, shaking his head. "I do this for my mom. It's called abstract art. I send them to her and she frames them and puts them up in her cubicle at work. I try to do one a month."

"So, you don't live with your mom, but you still talk to her?" I asked.

"Yep. Every week," Anton said. "When I did live with my mom in Chicago, we used to go to Lincoln Park Zoo all the time. She loved the giraffes."

"What was *your* favorite animal at the zoo?" I asked.

"Oh, mine? Promise not to laugh?" Anton said.

"What would be funny about – oh, just tell me," I said, grinning at what it might be.

"Alright then, here goes, my favorite animals at

the zoo were the pigs. There were these baby pigs at the petting zoo and they were just the cutest things I ever saw," he said. "They would come right up and shove their little pink noses in my hand and grunt and snort. Okay, you can laugh now."

"A pig is a farm animal, silly, not a zoo animal. And why would I laugh? They're super cute, and yummy, too," I said, through giggles.

"That's wrong, Jilly, so wrong," Anton said.

"Piglets by the way, baby pigs are called piglets," I informed him.

"Whatever, but they were so adorable – I don't eat bacon to this day," he said.

"Do you eat pork chops?" I asked him, laughing. He didn't get a chance to answer because *you know who* came walking over. What could Brianna and the look-alikes possibly want from us?

"Oh, isn't that cute, girls," she said to the look-alikes. "The two misfits found their way to each other. Are you two, like, a thing now?" she said in her super snotty way.

"Brianna, just back off, okay? We're just eating our lunch," Anton said.

"Oh, so you don't actually like Jillbilly then? Well, that makes more sense," she said, in a very know-it-all way.

"What do you want, Brianna?" I asked, as my irritation started to rise. I could feel my ears turning pink, just like Ms. Jenkins' ears on my first day.

"Did you hear something girls?" Brianna said. "Was I talking to her? I didn't think so." The look-alikes shook their bobble heads as if to say no.

"So, anyways, *Anton*, would you mind taking this back to Mr. Peterson for me? I'm leaving early today and I would really appreciate it," she said with a sickly sweet smile, and then handed him a book. "Thanks, you're a real hero, Anton."

With that, she was gone, she didn't even wait to see if he would say yes. UGH! She had managed to change my entire world, without even saying a single word to me. Why didn't Anton defend me when she called me Jillbilly? Why did he say we were just having lunch? Why, why, *why* didn't he do something different?

"Why would you take that for her, Anton?" I asked. I couldn't believe he would be so nice to her. "She's so – so – just mean. How could you do *anything* for that girl?"

"It's the polite thing to do, and you know that, Jilly," Anton said.

"No, I don't, and why did you tell her we were just having lunch?" I asked.

I didn't say more, but I felt betrayed by Anton. He was supposed to be *my* friend, not *hers*! I never even saw him talking to her before now. I thought for sure she was just tryin' to hurt my friendship with Anton.

"Jilly, I can tell by the way your cheeks are lit up that you're upset," Anton said. "In case you weren't listening, she insulted me, too. I just don't want to get into it with her. Why do you let her get to you?"

"Anton, I'm upset with you, not her – you didn't even say we were friends," I said. "As far as she knows, you were tutoring me or somethin' like that."

"Hold on a minute, Jilly, I didn't do anything wrong," Anton said. "I didn't ask her to come over. All I'm doing is bringing a book back to Mr. Peterson for her. What are you getting all worked up about?"

Oh no, I could feel it comin' on – I was gonna cry. I don't know why it happened, but sometimes, when I got really, really mad, I cried. I bit down on my lip real hard in the hopes it would distract my brain from startin' the tears. It didn't work.

"I gotta use the restroom, I'll be back," I said, as I grabbed all my stuff and took off towards the girls' room. I didn't go back. I didn't want to leave him sittin' there all alone, but I couldn't stop cryin' before lunch was over. After lunch, I went to the nurse and faked a headache so I could hide out in there. The nurse always let you lie down for a while if you told her you had a real bad headache. I needed my cry-face to fade before I saw Anton again.

As I laid there on the stiff orange cot, I thought about what I did, and I saw the stupid in it – after I did it – just like Daddy said. It all happened so fast there wasn't any time to stop and think about the unintended consequences before the words fell out of my mouth.

I wondered what the unintended consequences were going to be. As I thought about Anton and the possibility of him being mad at me, I started to cry again. The nurse asked me what was wrong. She suggested I call my mom, but we didn't have a phone, so that was out.

I thought of at least seven unintended consequences that could happen, and none of 'em were good. The one I feared the most was that Anton wouldn't want to be friends anymore. Another one was him and Brianna would end up becoming better friends than me and Anton, and I would have to watch it all happen. I couldn't even think about that one.

As I lay there on the cold, stiff cot in the nurse's office, I realized I blamed Anton, and it really wasn't his fault. I couldn't believe I did that. He was my first real friend, and now, I might have lost him. Way to go, *me*!

That day on the bus ride home, Anton sat in his old seat, in the back of the bus, without me. Yep, that was one of the unintended consequences I was hoping would not happen. I wished I could just sink right down into my seat on that bus and never have to see him again. I just couldn't bear to look at him after I broke our friendship and all. I was a real misfit again, with not even one friend.

THINK CRITICALLY...

- **Would you describe Brianna's actions as bullying? Why or why not?**
- **What do you do or say when someone bullies you?**
- **What do you do or say when someone bullies your friends?**
- **How do you feel or act when your friends are the ones doing the bullying?**

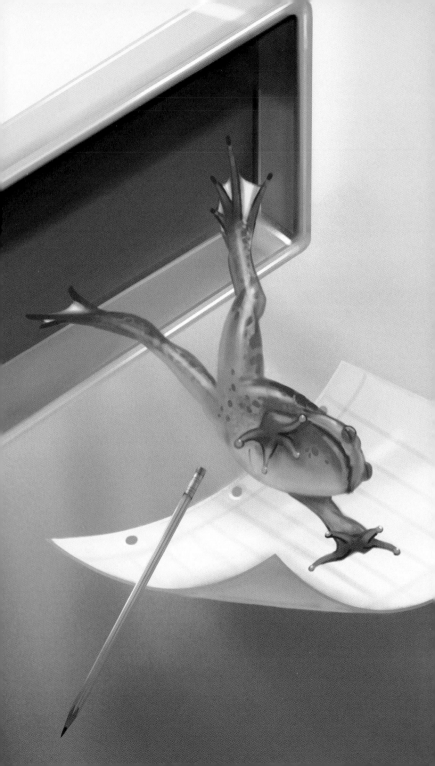

CHAPTER SEVEN
Green Frogs a Leapin'

It had been two days since my fight with Anton. That morning before school, I decided to talk to my mom about it. She suggested I make the first move if the friendship was important to me, and it definitely was. She also said I shouldn't expect him to apologize to me because he had to come to terms with what happened on his own, and just because one person was ready to apologize, didn't mean the other person was ready.

Him ignoring me on the bus was okay, but lunch, well that was a different story. Honestly, I hated sitting alone at lunch. Nothing made me feel more like I didn't belong in that stupid school than sitting all alone at a big table by myself. I tried to read, but I just couldn't help feeling like everyone was staring at me. There was always some teacher who felt sorry for me and tried to keep me company.

The truth was, I just plain missed him. He always made me smile and I missed smiling. I decided it was okay if he didn't apologize to me since I was probably the one who kinda' started the fight, and then ran off before we could talk about it. I was going to go right up to him at lunch that day and tell him I was sorry. Hopefully, he would apologize, too, but it was okay if he didn't.

There was only one more class until lunchtime, and I was gettin' nervous about going up to Anton, but he was my only real friend, so I figured it was worth it. But first, I had to get through frog dissection in biology. I was actually excited to get to see the insides of a frog.

Mr. Johnson was assigning pairs of students to work together, and I couldn't believe my ears. First, Mr. Johnson called my name, and then hers. What? Brianna!? No, I could not have heard him correctly.

"Excuse me, Mr. Johnson," Brianna said, in her perfect little voice. "Kelsie and I have already prepared for the lesson and we were planning on working together, so may I be re-assigned?"

"That's great you took the initiative to prepare ahead of class, Brianna," Mr. Johnson said, and I was hopeful he would agree. "But in real life, you don't always get to pick your team, so it's important you learn to work together with people outside of your usual friends."

"It's okay, Mr. Johnson, I don't mind working with someone else, *really*," I said in an effort to show him *I really did not* mind being partnered with someone else – *anyone else*!

"I'm sorry, Jilly, but I've already made my decision and there will be no changes made," he said kindly. "Now, go and select your *Rana Temporaria*, that's the scientific name for a frog, and get to a lab table with your partner. The dissection kits are already out. You will need to complete one sheet with your partner. I will be moving around the room to check your progress. I will answer any questions you have when I visit your table."

I could feel Brianna's beastiness as I approached the frogs. While all the other students were discussing which one they wanted, she grabbed one off the table and slammed it down on a lab tray. I decided I was just going to follow her lead and let her have her way. I couldn't believe how spoiled she was acting. She reminded me of my little sister when she threw a baby fit. I just wanted to get this over with as quickly as possible.

As we worked on the frog dissection, she told me to do all the dissecting, while she did all the writing. When Mr. Johnson came by our table, he suggested we switch places. I took over the writing, and she took over the dissecting. She did not appreciate this. As soon as Mr. Johnson walked away, Brianna grabbed the pencil out of my hand and shoved the forceps towards me.

"No, Brianna, Mr. Johnson said we needed to switch," I said firmly, shoving the forceps back at her.

"I don't care *what* he said, I'm not dissecting this nasty little frog," she said, as she shoved the entire tray, frog and all, right back at me.

"Oh no – I am not getting in trouble because of you!" I said. The other students by us started looking our way. "You are just a spoiled little brat afraid to get your perfect little fingers dirty, and I'm not *doing your work for you!*"

"Oh yeah?" she said, with her voice really loud. "Well, you're just a silly little country girl who probably doesn't even know how to spell, so I'm not letting *you* do the *writing*!"

That's when it happened. She shoved the tray to me and I pushed back, and then all of a sudden, *CRASH*! Our tray, frog and all, hit the ground, and Mr. Johnson came walking over, with a not-so-happy look on his face.

THINK CRITICALLY...

- How do Jilly and Brianna feel about working together?

- What things did the two girls do to make working together better? Worse?

- Have you ever had to work with someone you would rather not work with?

- What are some things you can do or say to make working with others easier for yourself and the other person?

NOTES TO SELF:

CHAPTER EIGHT
Crocodile Tears are Invisible

I could already feel the unintended consequences comin' my way. And yes, I saw the stupid as soon as I did it. What was wrong with me lately? It seemed as if some evil twin had taken over my body and mind and just made me do things I knew were wrong! I felt completely broken inside.

But wait, was she *crying*? Yes, she was. Brianna was crying, but there were no actual tears – crocodile tears, of course!

Before Mr. Johnson could actually send us to the principal, she ran out of the room – apparently to the principal's office. When I got there, a couple of minutes behind her, I heard her telling the principal that *I was the one who pushed it off the table*! Incredible.

I burst into his office and immediately began telling Mr. Michael what actually happened, even though I figured he wouldn't believe me. It didn't really matter because he said we would be taking our lunch in Mr. Johnson's room that day so we could finish our frog dissection. Yuck! Who wants to eat while they dissect a frog? But that wasn't even the worst of it.

Starting the next day, we – me and Brianna – had lunch detention together for a full week!

We had to eat *together* in a room by *ourselves*, in the counselor's office. This was going to be bad. I just knew it. He also said if we couldn't prove to him that we had solved our differences by the time our week was over, we were *both* going to miss the homecoming pep rally on Friday.

Personally, I would rather not go. But Brianna was a cheerleader, so missing the pep rally meant she wouldn't be able to cheer. *Good*! After she lied to Mr. Michael about me, I didn't care if she ever got to cheer again!

By this time, it was lunchtime, and Mr. Michael walked us down to the cafeteria and through the lunch line like kindergartners. Then, he walked us all the way to Mr. Johnson's room, where our frog was waiting on the floor with its guts spilled out. Wow, did it stink! I immediately started picking it up because I knew *she wouldn't*. So much for my lunch.

Touching those slimy frog's legs made me remember my daddy. He used to catch big frogs in the pond out back behind our old house. After he skinned 'em and cut their legs off, their legs would jump around. This made me giggle when I was a child. Apparently I giggled out loud thinking about it.

"What's so funny, *Jillbilly*?" Brianna asked between gritted teeth.

I tried to change the subject, "Brianna, what are you afraid of? A little ol' dead frog? He can't hurt you," I said.

"Mr. Johnson," she said. "She's laughing while we work. It's making it difficult for me to concentrate.

Could we just work alone please?"

"No," he said, as he walked over to check on our progress. "Is there something funny about dissection, Jilly? Why don't you tell me what you think is funny?"

I didn't want to lie, and besides, I couldn't think of a lie fast enough, so the truth just came tumbling out of my mouth.

"Well, I was just rememberin' my daddy, *rest his soul*, and how he would go giggin' in our pond during frog hunting season. After he cleaned the frogs and got 'em ready for the skillet, their legs would jump around."

"That's disgusting!" Brianna piped in, as she rolled her eyes like she did the first day we met. I wondered if it hurt to roll her eyes so far back in her head. It sure looked painful.

"So your father used to hunt frogs, is that right?" Mr. Johnson asked.

"Yes, sir, he liked to live off the land." I answered. Brianna just rolled her eyes.

"Frog's legs are considered a delicacy by many people around the world, and they're quite healthy," Mr. Johnson said. "Your dad must have been a smart man, Jilly. Do you know why the legs jumped around?"

"No, but it was funny," I said, and I smiled as I remembered how my daddy would sing and say he was making 'em dance to his tune.

"Well, actually the reason the muscles twitch, is due to science," he said, as he went to his computer and pulled up a video. He had me and Brianna come over to his desk so we could learn about how the salt worked with the ATP, whatever that is, in the frog's muscles to make them jump like that.

"So now you know the science behind why the legs twitched," he said, seemingly satisfied with himself. I preferred my daddy's explanation, but I still appreciated Mr. Johnson's more scientific reasoning.

"Gross," Brianna said, as she flipped her hair and washed her hands for the third time. This made Mr. Johnson laugh.

I don't know why, but I felt better now, even though I never did get to tell Anton I was sorry. That would have to wait until another time. I didn't want to tell him on the bus because there were too many kids around. I'd have to figure something out, and soon, because I knew he'd want to know what happened with Brianna.

THINK CRITICALLY...

- Do you think Jilly and Brianna will ever work out their differences?

- What do you think can be done to make Jilly and Brianna's relationship better?

- Should Jilly keep trying to work things out with Brianna or is she better off avoiding her classmate?

NOTES TO SELF:

CHAPTER NINE
Dirt Roads are Brown

The next day was like any other, except I had to have lunch with Brianna, which was actually okay. We didn't talk to each other – not even once. As we left the counselor's office, Mrs. Barry reminded us we needed to work out our differences. She asked if we wanted help working through our issues. We both said "no" to that.

In study hall that afternoon, I finished all of my homework for the day. It was Friday, and I planned on going over to Anton's over the weekend so we could finally get this stupid fight over with. By the time school was over, I was ready to go home. I was thinking I might take Kaylie down to the river to look for more rocks for the rock garden.

As I walked down the pathway to our old house, I could see Mom and Kaylie in the yard. She rarely got outside anymore. Mom looked like an angel in the sunlight. Her and Kaylie were planting rocks in the rock garden. Kaylie came running over to me and asked me to take Mom to the dump.

After I put my backpack in the house, me, Mom and Kaylie headed down the old, worn path towards the dump. It looked different from when I first walked it. Now, instead of being covered in thick, green grasses, the grass had turned brown and there were leaves dotting it here and there. Mom said Mother Nature was getting ready for winter. I wondered what winter would be like up north. We never got much snow when we lived in southern Missouri.

"So, have you found anything interesting in the old dump?" Mom asked.

"Yeah, I've found lots of bottles, an old milk can, and lots of old forks – just stuff like that," I told her.

"You know, Jilly, some of those old things could be worth money," she said.

"I know – I was hoping we could find a flea market or a shop where we could sell some of them," I said. "But I really want to keep some of the bottles. It's too bad the prettiest ones are broken."

"Speaking of broken, did you manage to fix your relationship with Anton? What did he say when you apologized for walking out on him during lunch?" Mom asked.

"I didn't exactly get to do that, yet," I said, secretly hoping she wouldn't ask why!

"Why not?" Mom asked, of course.

"Because I got in trouble, that's why," I just came out with it. "Now I have to eat lunch in the counselor's office with another girl."

"What? When? Why didn't you tell me?" Mom wondered.

I told Mom all about what happened and I thought she would be really mad at me, but it turns out, she was very understanding of the situation. She even gave me some advice on how to work out my differences with Brianna. She also helped me understand if I didn't help Brianna get to that pep rally, things would probably get a lot worse for me in the long run. I had to think about that. I didn't want to help her, but I didn't want to make things worse, either.

"Mom, could I walk down to Anton's when we get back home?" I asked. "I really want to get on with things. I won't see him at school again until next Friday."

"How far away is it?" she asked.

"It's not far, and I will be back before dark," I promised her.

"Okay, I guess you're old enough to walk a country road," she said.

"Can I go now?" I asked.

"Go ahead," she said. "I'll finish up here with your sister. Just be back before dark, you hear?"

"Yes, I promise! Thanks, Mom," I said, as I ran towards the house and road. I ran all the way until I ran out breath, before I walked.

As I walked along the old dirt road to Anton's house, I thought about all the ways things could go wrong. What if he was still mad? What if he didn't want to be friends anymore? What if, what if, what if? Oh, the what if's were killing me! I could smell the dusty road under my shoes and I thought about turning back and going home at least seven times during the 20-minute walk to his house. But I didn't turn back. He was my friend and I needed to make things right.

I got up to his driveway and I could see two people in the yard. It looked like they were painting a bench of some sort. I didn't see Anton anywhere.

I figured this was my last chance to turn tail and run, but I knew our friendship might depend on me doing this. Deep down, I was afraid he wouldn't forgive me, even though I knew he was a good person.

"Hi, is Anton here?" I asked the nice, older couple working on the bench.

"He's in the house. You have a name, young lady?" the man asked.

"I'm sorry, I'm, uh, Jilly. It's nice to meet you, Mr…"

"I'm George, and this here is Lou," he said as he pointed to his wife. She wiped her hands on a rag she had attached to her pants and shook my hand. She had a kind smile.

"Go on in there, Jilly," Lou said. "He's playing video games with his brother. You just go on in," she said.

"Okay, thanks," I said, as I walked towards the door. I could hear them laughing and playing as I walked up on the porch. Once again, I wanted to run home, but I just went in there.

"Hi, Anton. Um, can I talk to you?" I said.

"Jilly? What are you doing here?" Anton said, clearly shocked that I was there.

"Can I just talk to you outside for a minute? It'll just be a minute, I swear," I said. I don't know why, but it felt like my heart was beating faster.

"What?" he said as he walked out onto the porch.

"I'm sorry. I really acted like a, um, a…"

"Na, na, na – Jilly, don't say anything. I should not have let her treat you like that. I should be the one to say I'm sorry, so, I'm sorry," he said, and made a kind of half smile.

"No, Anton, I acted like, like my sister Kaylie when she doesn't get her way. I understand what you were saying. Brianna was wrong – not you," I said.

There, it was over, at last!

"I was feeling pretty bad and I wanted to say something to you, but you just looked so hurt and mad that I was afraid to go up to you. I can't believe you came all the way over here to apologize. Now I really feel like a jerk," he said, looking a bit like a hurt puppy.

"It's okay, really," I said, "Anton – can we just forget this ever happened?"

"Deal. Hey, you want to play with us?" he asked.

"Sure, I ain't ever played before, but I could learn," I said.

"You never played Fighter Knights, or you never played video games before?" his brother asked, incredulously, as if either answer I gave was still going to shock him.

"Video games," I said.

"This ought to be fun!" Anton said.

"More, like *funny*," his brother said, already laughing.

While we played, I told Anton all about my trouble with Brianna. We played video games until his aunt and uncle came in, and then I realized it was getting dark. They asked if I was staying for dinner?

"Oh no! I better get home. I didn't realize how late it had gotten – my mom's gonna be worried," I said, as I hurried towards the door.

"I can drive you home while Lou puts dinner out," his uncle said. "It's not good to go out walking around after dark, especially not for a young girl like yourself."

"Thank you, Mr…," I started to say.

"George, just George," he answered.

Soon, we were driving down the old dirt road in George's old work truck. The dust swirled around in the sunlight. I could taste the dust in my mouth.

"So, is your daddy going to come out yelling if I drive in your driveway?" George asked.

"No, sir, I don't have a daddy anymore, least not on earth," I said.

"And your mother is okay with you hanging around with Anton?" he asked, in all seriousness.

"Of course, why wouldn't she be?" I said.

"Because there's still a lot of folks that don't approve of their kids hanging around with people who are different than they are."

"Oh, my gosh, *no*, my mom's *not* one of those people, I can assure you of that, George!"

"Well, that's good to know," he said, as he laughed a little.

"Here we are," I said, as he pulled up to my driveway.

"Here we are," he said, back to me real slow.

He didn't say anything else, so I got out of the truck and walked in the house. Mom was cleaning up dinner. She was a little mad I was late, but not much. I figured I better try to talk to Sam tonight, if I had time. A lot happened that day.

Dear Sam,

I finally made up with Anton. He was really good about it. I just wish I hadn't waited so long to do it. We played video games and had a good time. We made plans for him to come over to my house this weekend. He said he wanted to pick through the dump and get some broken glass for a project he was working on with his uncle. Broken glass? Oh well, I was glad the pretty glass bottles were going to be used for something. He didn't tell me what.

Things are not getting any better at Blue Creek Middle School, but I didn't expect they would. I think I will try talking to Brianna next week when we're eating lunch together, to see if we can figure out a way to work out our differences. Besides, Anton said I could sit with him at the pep rally if I was able to go, so now I have a reason to want to go.

Remember how I told you about seeing something in the woods? I saw it again when I went in with my mom today. I'm going to show it to Anton when he comes over tomorrow.

Till next time,

 Jilly

THINK CRITICALLY...

- The dump has become a special place for Jilly. Why do you think an old dump full of broken things has become such a special place for Jilly?
- Who are the people in Anton's family?
- How is Anton's family the same or different from your family?

NOTES TO SELF:

CHAPTER NINE

CHAPTER TEN
Gray Day

"Jill-eeee!" Mom said from the living room. "Someone's at the door!"

"Getting it, Mom," I shouted back from my room upstairs. I wondered why Anton had come over so early in the morning. He knocked again. I looked at the clock in the kitchen – it wasn't even eight o'clock yet.

"Coming," I shouted.

I opened the door and there he was. Anton was smiling wide and holding a bucket and a shovel. He had gloves for me and Kaylie, and a pair of boots for me, all shoved in the bucket. He carried all that stuff from his house so we wouldn't get hurt diggin' in the dump. He was so thoughtful, that was one of my favorite things about him. We put on our gear and headed off down the path. As usual, Kaylie came with us. She was real excited she could actually dig in the dump this time – thanks to Anton!

The sky was a pale gray that day. It was almost as if it wanted to rain, but Mother Nature just wouldn't let it happen. The clouds were thick and low, the wind was calm, and the air smelled like fresh cut grass. I really hoped it wouldn't rain because I wanted to show Anton what I had found in the woods.

When we were almost there, I secretly pointed to Anton to look at the mysterious thing I found. He got my hint and kept quiet. He saw it. He told me and Kaylie he had to go "take a leak." Kaylie laughed when I told her what that meant. Soon, he was back at the dump.

"It looks like an old traveling wagon," he said. "It would make a fine hangout, if we fixed it up – what do you think?"

"I haven't actually checked it out yet – I wanted to do it when I was alone, without *you know who*," I said, pointing to Kaylie behind her head.

"Well, I can watch her, you should go check it out right now," Anton suggested. He got Kaylie's attention and kept her distracted so I could go check out the thing in the woods. I ran off and started my investigation.

It was the coolest thing I had ever seen. It had big metal wheels and an old wood stove inside. It was a little lopsided where it had sunk into the ground, but other than that, it seemed to be usable for a hangout. There was even a little old table and two chairs inside. It would be just right for me and Anton! When I got back, Anton was telling Kaylie to pick out only the prettiest broken glass, and put it in the bucket.

"So, what exactly are you going to do with all that broken glass and metal?" I asked him.

"I'm going to make art," he said.

"Art, huh? What kind of art?" I asked. I was feeling a little suspicious because I felt like he was hiding something from me.

"Secret art, that's what kind," he said, with a big silly smile on his face.

"Well then, how am I supposed to know what you're looking for if you don't tell me what you're doin?" I asked, trying hard to get it out of him.

"Na, na, na, you won't be able to get me to tell you like that. I *said* it was a secret," he said. "You just pick out the shiniest, brightest pieces of broken glass, and put them in the bucket. You think you can do that?"

"On one condition," I said, with my finger in the air. "You gotta promise to show me when you're done."

"Deal," he said.

"I have one!" Kaylie said, excitedly, holding up a bright purple piece of glass.

"Wow, Kaylie, that looks just like the bottle I found for you. Do you still have it?" he asked.

"Yes, I do – I'm never gonna lose it – I promise! Will you use this one in your art project, Anton?" a wide-eyed Kaylie asked.

"Of course I will. It will be the most special piece," he said, as he smiled down at her.

Kaylie grinned ear-to-ear as she carefully placed the bright purple glass chip into Anton's bucket. We spent the better part of the morning looking through the dump for broken glass and metal. Afterwards, Anton and I carried all the old bottles I found earlier up to the house. After Anton left, I spent a long time looking at the bottles, washing them out, and thinking about what I could do with them.

The gray clouds disappeared as the sun rose high above the old farm. I realized I had been out there for hours. My growling stomach reminded me I hadn't eaten anything that day. I figured I better go in the house before Mom came looking for me.

When I got in, Mom was layin' on the kitchen floor, not moving. Kaylie was sitting there, crying at her side. There was a tiny trickle of blood on her forehead and it ran down to the old gray tiles on the floor.

"Mom, Mom – can you hear me? Mom!" I shouted, but she didn't move. Was she dead? I checked her breathing and she was still alive, but she wasn't moving.

"Kaylie, what happened? Why didn't you come get me?" I asked.

"I tried, Jilly, but I couldn't find you. Momma just fell down and I don't know why, Jilly, but I think she's dead," Kaylie said through her sobs.

"No, she not's dead, Kaylie. She's going to be okay. I'm just sure of it. Stop crying, okay?! You've got to be a big girl right now and watch Momma while I go get help, okay. Okay? Can you do that?" I asked.

"Yes, Jilly, I can do that," Kaylie said, trying hard not to cry.

I ran all the way to Anton's house down the dusty old road and found George working in the yard.

"George, can you call an ambulance, please? My mom is lying on the floor in the kitchen – she's hurt," I yelled. He said he would come down and take her to the hospital, if she needed to go. George grabbed his cell phone, then we all – me, Lou, and George – got in

Lou's car, and headed straight for my house. Mom was still on the floor when we got there. She was awake now. She was a little confused, but said she tripped over one of Kaylie's toys and she must have hit her head pretty hard.

George decided to take Mom to the hospital to have her checked out. He asked if me and Kaylie had anywhere to go or anyone to call while Mom was at the hospital. We didn't, so he suggested we pile in the car to go to the hospital with Mom. Everything in that hospital was gray from the floors to the walls, and even the ceilings.

Please don't let her die, I thought to myself. I couldn't stand to lose another parent. Kaylie would be taken away, and I would have to go live with strangers. And then I started worrying that if Momma was really bad off… or even if she wasn't, if one of the doctors asked the wrong questions and found out that Momma still gets so sad and sick sometimes… would they take Kaylie away anyway? I was really, really scared, but I had to be brave for my little sister.

I played games with Kaylie in the large gray waiting room to take her mind off of things. Lou and George stayed with us while the doctor checked out Mom. I was grateful they were there – it was scary enough having to think about all of this.

While I played with Kaylie, I got to thinking about what life would be like if Mom could take care of herself like Lou and George do. I thought about how just the other day she took that long walk with us to the dump. I thought about how she seemed to be getting better – even asking about my day, and giving good advice. And that's when I decided, if Mom is okay, then I would darn sure make certain she stays that way. I would figure out how to do that.

After a while, the doctor came out and talked to us. He said Mom had a concussion, but she was going to be okay. She just needed to take it easy. He gave Mom and me some signs to watch out for, and then George and Lou drove us home.

THINK CRITICALLY...

- Jilly's mom is hurt and goes to the hospital. How would you describe Jilly's relationship with Uncle George and Aunt Lou after the hospital?

- If Jilly were to write in her journal at the end of this chapter, what do you think she would tell SAM?

NOTES TO SELF:

CHAPTER ELEVEN
Grandmas are Glorious

Monday morning came around all too soon. Lou offered to check on Mom and Kaylie while I was at school. I sure was glad Anton's aunt was our neighbor, otherwise, I woulda' had to stay home with Mom.

The first half of the day went by really fast. I was not looking forward to having lunch with Brianna again. UGGGH! I decided I would make the first move since she clearly was not going to, even if I had to pretend to be nice to her. When I walked into the counselor's office with my lunch tray, Brianna was already in there with her bag lunch. She always had the best stuff from home.

"Hi," I said, but she just gave me a dirty look. Expected. "I think we need to talk about how we get out of this before the pep rally Friday," I said. "What do you think?"

"What do you care?" Brianna asked. She looked like she had just eaten a sour pickle – the kind that makes your nose crinkle.

"I don't care, but I know *you* do, and since it doesn't matter to me, then you should care all that much more!" I said. "So, do you wanna make a plan to get out of here, or what?"

"Whatever," she said, as if she couldn't bear the thought of talkin' to me.

"Well, we have to make it believable, or Mrs. Barry will not buy it," I said.

"You have my attention," she said, with a golden eyebrow raised high.

"Here's my idea," I said, and then I told her all about how we could help each other with our homework and Mrs. Barry would think we were getting along. Brianna agreed it was a good idea. Our plan was sure to work. I helped her with her biology homework that day. Okay, I basically did it for her, and she was supposed to help me with my English paper. We were actually getting along pretty good, but I wasn't getting my hopes up.

Lunch was over before we knew it and our plan was working nicely. Mrs. Barry bought it hook, line, and sinker. The next day came and Brianna never showed up. Turns out, she stayed home sick that day – and the day after that. On Thursday, our last day, we were still getting along really good. I wasn't sure who tricked who more. Did we trick Mrs. Barry and Mr. Michael into believing we were getting along, or did they trick us into actually getting along?

Brianna told me she felt bad because she couldn't help me with my English paper. She asked if I wanted her to look it over and edit it for me. I took it out of my backpack and I gave it to her. I thought we had really crossed a line into possible friendship.

It was *possible*, right?

The next day was the pep rally. On my way to the gym, Brianna actually smiled at me when we passed in the hallway. I smiled back. Anton just rolled his eyes – so did the look-alikes. I sat down with Anton and his friends in the bleachers. Trina, one of the girls Anton knew, handed me one of her pom-poms and we cheered, clapped, and stomped our feet 'til it sounded like the bleachers were going to cave in! All thanks to the cheerleaders, like Brianna, and the look-alikes, who kept us going strong! I guess I was glad Brianna got to cheer.

"So, are you going to the homecoming game tonight?" Anton asked me.

"No, it's not really my thing," I said.

"What do you mean it's not your *thing*?" Anton asked. "It's homecoming, Jilly, it's everyone's *thing*."

"I don't have a ride," I said. "And besides, I don't think my mom would let me go, 'specially after what happened last weekend."

"That was pretty scary, but your mom's better now," he said. "You could ride with me. I'm sure Aunt Lou wouldn't mind driving you – she's driving Trina and Marcus. Come on, Jilly – say you'll go."

"Well, okay, you can come by the house on your way," I said. "And if my mom says it's alright, I'll go." I was pretty sure my mom would not let me go, but it was worth a try.

"Alright, cool – see you later, then," he said. He was all smiles when we left the gymnasium after the pep rally. I couldn't wait to find out if I could go! The bus ride home seemed to take forever that day.

When I finally got home, there was a shiny Chrysler parked in the driveway. It was really pretty and it had Minnesota license plates. I wondered whose it was.

When I walked in the house, there was an older lady sitting at the table – she looked very nice. Her hair was fire-orange – just like Daddy's use to be. Her nails were painted purply-pink, her shirt was covered in splashes of colors, and her pants were turquoise. I imagined if she was in her car, she'd make a full rainbow. She was drinking coffee with mom and they both looked up at me, kind of strange-like. This was a very curious woman.

"Jilly, this is your grandmother, Roxie," Mom said, kind of quiet. "She is your father's mother. I had Lou call her last week after I left the hospital. I thought it was best for you to meet her – and to get to know her, you know, in case we ever need her."

"*Grandmother*?" I asked. I could not believe that I had a grandmother. A grandmother I never knew? And where had she been all these years? I just couldn't even believe it. And how did she get here, I mean, obviously she drove the car, but this was just weird.

"Why are you here? I mean, where were you *before*, like when Daddy *died*? I mean no disrespect, but I just want to know, that's all," I said.

"Jilly, please, your grandmother… " was all Mom got out before the grandmother lady interrupted her.

"It's okay, Yvonne, let me explain it to her," the brightly-colored woman said to Mom, and then she turned to me. "Jillian, your father and I didn't talk much. His father raised him. I wanted to be a part of his life, but he did not want me to be in it. That was his right. Sometimes families don't stay together, Jillian."

"It's Jilly, *please*," I said. "But I don't understand why I never met you before now."

"Because I was respecting your father's wishes, that's why – plain and simple. Your father was a very proud man, just like his father, and he, for whatever reason, did not want me interfering in his life, so I complied. I am sorry, but, with your permission I would like to be in your life now – if you'll let me," she spoke as if she was unsure if I was okay with that.

"Of course you can, yes, that would be great!" I dropped my backpack on the floor and threw my arms around her. She seemed a little nervous.

"Well, what do you say I take us all out to dinner tonight?" she asked.

"That's not necessary," Mom said.

"I *insist*, Yvonne," the older, grandmother lady said to my mom. Mom gave in and since she insisted, that meant I wasn't going to the homecoming game, so I didn't even bother telling them about it.

When Anton showed up with his Aunt Lou, my grandmother *insisted* I go to the game with *them*. She was a little confusing and very *insistful*, but I was happy I got to go the game. She said she would take me out for a one-on-one lunch the next day so we could catch up on everything that had happened since I was born. Wow. That will be a long conversation, I thought. Then she gave me ten dollars spending money for the game!

That night at the game, I got to know Anton's friends – more misfits, just like me, well, like me, but different. My favorite was Trina, who was very smart.

In fact, she was in classes with mostly seventh-graders, and some eighth-graders, too. She said it made her feel different because she didn't get to know a lot of the kids in her own grade, and that the older kids didn't seem to want to get to know her. I liked her, even though she was a lot smarter than me. I kind of wished I was too smart for my grade.

Trina told me all about the school dance that was coming up. It was the Blue Creek Middle School Fall Dance. It was pretty exciting because I had never been to a school dance before. Trina said she was going with some other girls from school. I wondered if Anton would invite me?

THINK CRITICALLY...

- Early in the chapter, Jilly tries to work things out with Brianna. Do you think Jilly's efforts will result in an improved relationship with Brianna? Why or why not?

- Jilly discovers she has a grandmother and she makes a new friend, Trina. How could having these new people in her life change things for her?

- Do you believe it is important to have family and friends? Why?

NOTES TO SELF:

CHAPTER TWELVE
Her First Dress was Ice Blue

The next day was crazy fun. My new grandmother took me out to lunch at a really fancy restaurant. We talked about everything under the sun. I couldn't figure out why my daddy did not want this wonderful woman in his life. I, for one, thought she was utterly fascinating. She talked my ear off about how she lived in three different countries during her life and how she settled down on a big farm in Minnesota that was only five hours from where we lived. She even said I could come visit her some time. I ate so much I thought I might pop.

"What about dessert?" she asked.

"I am pretty sure my belly's gonna bust, Gr...," and then I realized I didn't have a cool grandmother name for her. "What do you want me to call you?"

"Whatever you want, you can call me Roxie, or Grandma, or Grandma Roxie, whatever you prefer," she said.

"Okay, how about Grams?" I said.

"Grams it is!" we decided.

"What about school – how is school going, Jilly? Your mom told me you just moved to a new school," she said. "Tell me all about it."

"Well, yeah, we move a lot since Dad, you know, passed, an' all," I said.

"Yes, I understand your mother loved your father very much," Grams said. "It must have been very difficult for her, and for you, as well."

"Yes, ma'am – I mean, Grams," I said.

"But what about you now? Do you have a best friend or a boyfriend?" she asked.

"Ha! Right – that's funny, Grams!" I said, laughing.

"Why is that funny?" she asked. "You're smart and funny, and I bet any boy would be glad to snatch you up."

"Well, no, I've never really had a boyfriend, or a best friend for that fact, but there is a dance coming up soon, and I was thinking that someone might ask me," I said. "I mean, I wouldn't go, but it would be nice to be asked." I figured I may as well be honest with her. I wasn't sure what kind of stuff you talked about with your grandmother.

"A dance? Oh, I remember school dances," Grams said.

"Well, this is the Blue Creek Middle School Fall Dance," I said. "It's a big deal, I guess."

"What if your, uh, friend, asks you – do you have something to wear?" she asked.

"No, but Mom wouldn't let me go anyway," I said. "Her car isn't running right now."

"I thought the person who did the asking had to arrange transportation. Have times changed that much?" Grams asked, as she shook her head back and forth.

"Well, no, but I guess I didn't really think about

it," I said, between laughs. I felt a little silly not actually knowing something like that, but I guess it made sense.

"Well, how about we go dress shopping, just in case?" she said.

"What? Really?" I could've screamed. I was not a girly girl, but I never really owned a pretty dress, and it might be good to have one on hand, just in case. "But, what if he doesn't ask me, Grams, and the dress goes to waste?"

"Then, you'll figure out somewhere else to wear it, but my guess is, you'll find a way to go to that dance," she said. "Besides, better safe than sorry is what I always say."

"Well, that sounds good to me," I said, as I popped up out of my seat in the big red booth. I was suddenly ready to leave and go dress shopping!

We went to every store in the mall. I must have tried on 30 dresses. I felt like Cinderella, and Grams was my fairy godmother, helping me out before the dance! My dress even looked like Cinderella's with ice blue satin and white frosting around the edges. It reminded me of a blue sky with only a few white clouds dancing around. It was beautiful.

After buying the dress, Grams said I needed shoes to match, so we went shoe shopping next. Then she got me some jewelry to match the shoes. The shoes and the jewelry were silver and sparkly. I could've peed I was so happy. I didn't think the day could get any better.

On our way home, Grams pulled into a shopping center, and we walked right into a cell phone store, and she bought me *and* Mom our very own cell phones! Mom was going to be so happy – I just knew she would. I couldn't wait to get home to give it to her.

"Now, Jilly, your mother may not appreciate me buying these phones," she said. "So you tell her you are going to work them off, okay? I expect you to come out to my farm next summer and paint a barn with me, you hear?"

"Of course, yes, I will!" I said.

"Well then, it's settled," Grams said. "So your mother cannot go getting all mad at me, okay? They're on my account so she doesn't have to worry about paying anything for them, but you follow her rules with your phone, understand?"

"Yes, ma'am, er, Grams!" I said.

I was so excited to have my own phone, just like everyone else. Even Anton had his own phone. With the dress, and the phone, and a grandmother – I finally felt like a normal kid, I think. I mean, the truth is, I didn't know what normal felt like, but if this is what normal felt like, I was okay with it.

When she drove up to the house, Mom and Kaylie were playing outside. Mom was NOT happy with the phones, or the dress and stuff, but she eventually gave in when Grams pointed out to her that she hurt herself just the week before, and we didn't have a way to call for help.

"Yvonne, I know how hard it is, but don't go making it harder on yourself and the girls over pride," she said. "It's not worth it. I'm glad you had Lou call me. I plan to treat both of the girls like my own grandchildren, if you will just let me. They need family, Yvonne, and you know it. Please, just let me do this one little thing, for them." Grams nearly begged her.

"Alright, then, but as soon as I get back to work, I will pay you back. I need a phone to get a job, but I have every intention of paying you back, Roxie," Mom insisted.

"Already taken care of, right, Jilly?" Grams said, looking directly at me.

"Yep, Grams asked me if I would come and paint a barn for her over the summer, to pay for the phones," I said. "And if it's okay with you, Mom, I would very much like to do that."

"Well, it seems like the two of you have it all worked out, then, don't you?" Mom said.

"Looks like we do. Now, Jilly, I'm leaving tomorrow," Grams said. "You use that phone to call me if you ever need anything, you hear me?"

I promised Grams I would call her if I ever needed her. I was really going to miss her!

THINK CRITICALLY...

- Jilly and her grandmother get to know one another in this chapter.
  How have things changed for Jilly?
- How do you think this relationship changed Jilly's perception of herself as a misfit?

CHAPTER THIRTEEN
Sunsets are Brilliant

Monday morning came like lightning. I woke up to my mom and Kaylie screaming their heads off downstairs. I jumped out of my bed and ran downstairs as fast as I could. They were runnin' around the kitchen, chasing a squirrel, or it was chasin' them – I couldn't tell who was chasing who. Mom was running around with a broom and Kaylie was bangin' pots and pans together. It was the funniest thing I ever did see.

The door was wide open and the crisp morning air was filling up the kitchen. Brrr! But Mr. Squirrel wasn't going anywhere. He was chattering and squawking like I ain't ever heard before. I was laughing so hard I cried. Mom was not happy with my laughing, or with Mr. Squirrel. We had quite a time getting that wild beast out of the old farmhouse that morning. It definitely woke me up!

Good thing Mom had her new phone because she called the landlord right away and told him he better come out and make sure that squirrel didn't make it inside again. He told Mom he'd be out later that week to seal off any squirrel holes in the roof. By the time the bus came that morning, I was ready to start my day, thanks to Mr. Squirrel waking me up so early.

As soon as I got to school, the first person I saw was Brianna. At least we were getting along now. I decided to say hi to her since we seemed to be friends now.

"Hi, Brianna. Did you have a chance to look at my English paper?" I asked her.

"Yes, I did," she said, really extra-sweet like. "It was really good so I went ahead and put it in Mr. Contin's inbox for you, when I turned mine in." As she said it, the look-alikes laughed. She just shot them a dirty look.

"Thanks for that," I said back to her, even though her friends were being rude.

"Okay – I'll catch you later," she said.

"I might actually be able to be her friend someday," I thought to myself.

Nothing unusual or fun happened that morning at school, and it was finally comin' up on lunchtime when I would get to see Anton. I figured if I told him all about the dress and all, he would get the hint I wanted to go to the dance with *him*.

I didn't get the chance to talk to him after all. On my way to the lunchroom, I saw Mr. Michael. He came right up to me and asked me to accompany him to the office.

"What's going on?" I asked. I was sure I hadn't done anything wrong.

"Cheating, that's what, Miss Hicklenbilly, cheating," he said, sounding angry.

"Cheating? Who cheated, and why am *I the one* going to the office?" I demanded. After all, I might've been a lot, but I wasn't a cheater.

"We will discuss it in my office," he said.

Everyone saw me going to the office with Mr. Michael. I was very confused because I had *no idea* what he was talking about. When I got there, Brianna was sitting outside his office, crying, as usual. Thinking we were friends and all, I asked her what was going on.

"Like you really don't know, *Jillbilly*!" she shouted viciously, kinda like a wild animal.

"What? No – I don't know what's going on. And *stop calling me that, Brianna!, It's JILLY*!" I yelled.

"You stole my homework while we were in lunch detention, and you know it!" she screamed like a pig squealin' in a loading chute. Even still, I could tell he believed *her*!

"Wait – I did no such thing, Mr. Michael, I do *not* know what she's talking about," I said, but he was not listening.

"In my office girls, both of you, *NOW*," he shouted. After we got in his office, he started again, "I am not interested in whether you two get along or not, what I am interested in is how you both ended up turning in *the exact same homework assignment* to Mr. Contin, because someone's *cheating*. And before you answer, know this, Jillian, Brianna turned hers in *first*."

"But Mr. Michael, Brianna was going to edit mine for me, *that's all*, and then she said she turned it in – this is just a mistake," I said. "Brianna, did you accidentally turn in two copies of yours to Mr. Contin?" I asked, sincerely trying to figure out exactly what happened.

"I did no such thing. Why would I edit *your* paper? I hate you, *Jillbilly,*" she said. "You can't do your own paper and you stole mine!"

There was no mistake. Clearly, she lied, and set me up, pretending to be nice to me the entire time! Wow.

"Mr. Michael, *she's lying*! She is *lying*, I tell you, *you have to believe me*!" I pleaded with him.

"Well, tell me what your paper was about, please, Jillian," he said.

"There's no point," I said. "She just lied and there's nothing I can do about it, so whatever, but I will say this, *I did not* steal her work, *I would not* steal her work – you – you can't let her get away with this," I begged Mr. Michael, but he did not listen.

"Mr. Michael," Brianna said, through her crocodile tears. "I can prove the work was mine. I sent a copy to Mr. Contin before we even went to lunch detention, which *proves* it was *my work she* copied!"

"You are a liar, Brianna Maples!" I shouted.

"Now girls, calm down, both of you," Mr. Michael said. "Brianna, you can go back to lunch. Jillian, you're going to spend the rest of the day in my office writing your *own paper*. I will also be putting in a call to your mother. This type of behavior will not be tolerated here, Jillian. I do not think you'll be attending the dance this year."

Suddenly, Mom having a phone didn't seem so great. I had to get Mr. Michael to believe me.

"I *did* my *own* paper, *Mr. Michael,*" I said. "I'll be glad to re-write it, but you are wrong about me. I do not deserve this and I *don't steal other people's work. Period.*"

I grabbed my notebook and started writing. I couldn't believe what had happened. How could she have lied so easily to me, and to Mr. Michael? Unbelievable.

My mom was going to kill me. Oh well, at least if that happened, I would not have to go back to Blue Creek Middle School.

That day on the bus ride home, I told Anton all about what happened with Brianna. He told me about some kids that were making fun of him in PE that day. I told him my mom said the only reason people tried to hurt other people's feelings is because they didn't feel good about their own self. He agreed. We decided we wouldn't talk about it, or think about it, anymore.

Besides, he was coming over again today and we needed to make plans. We decided we would go down to the old wagon and start fixin' it up. That's if my mom would still let me after she heard what happened.

When I got home, Mom was at the kitchen table, waiting for me. Kaylie was in the living room playing with the dolls Grams let me buy for her. I immediately started crying and telling her all about my day.

"Mom, I did not cheat. I would never do that, I *promise*," I said. "Mr. Michael was wrong about what he said."

"Tell me what happened, Jilly," she said softly.

I told her all about it. I also told her about how I was hoping Anton would ask me to the dance and that now I couldn't go, and I managed to keep crying the entire time I talked.

"Okay, okay – Jilly, calm down," she said. "There's nothing you can do about it now. I will talk with Mr. Michael to see if he will let you go to the dance."

"It's okay, Mom," I said. "I don't even want to go now, but thanks for believing me."

"Well, you can't let her win, Jilly," Mom said. "You need to go and let her know you are not going to let her get to you. You got that?"

"Yeah, I'll think about it. I love you, Mom," I said.

"You, too, darling," she replied. "And remember, as your daddy used to say, this too *shall pass*."

That was just another way of sayin' things couldn't get much worse, so hold on 'til they get better. Just then, Anton knocked on the door. He had his bucket, gloves, and boots. He said he needed some more glass for his art project. We headed out to the dump. We also wanted to get working on our new hideaway.

"Sorry about what happened with you and Brianna," Anton said.

"You mean Brianna the Beast?" I asked, not expecting an answer. "Well, don't be sorry because it ain't your fault. I mostly care about what my mom thinks. I just didn't want her to think I cheated – I would never steal someone else's work."

"Did she believe you?" he asked.

"Yeah, it's all good," I said. "She's going to talk to Mr. Michael to try to straighten things out."

"My uncle would have me doing chores for a

month and he wouldn't have believed me – you're lucky, you know, having your mom around all the time. I miss my mom," he said.

"You don't get to see her at all?" I asked.

"Na, na, na – that's not it," he said. "Yeah, I get to see her every summer, and some holidays, but I wish I had her around every day. Aunt Lou is nice to talk to, but I just miss my mom."

"Yeah, I hear ya' – I miss my dad all the time and he's been gone for almost six years now. When he first died, I thought I would forget him, but, I didn't," I said, as I smiled at him. "Can I ask what mistake your mom made that you can't live with her anymore?"

"No, you can't," he said quite seriously.

"I'm sorry," I quickly said.

"Jilly, of course you can ask," he laughed, as he shook his head at me. "The only mistake she made was helping my oldest brother. He actually did some bad stuff and my mom covered up for him. She didn't want him to get in trouble, but she ended up getting in trouble. In the end, we had to come here to live with Aunt Lou and Uncle George. My oldest brother – the one who should have gotten in trouble – still lives there by my mom – not fair, huh?"

"Wow – your mom was protecting your brother – how cool is that?" I said.

"Jilly, you're crazy," Anton said. "But in a good way."

"I don't even think I have an aunt or an uncle," I said. "I just found out I have a grandma, though. I call her Grams. I think it's really cool that you have so many people who love you enough to care for you."

"Can I ask you a question?" Anton asked me.

"Sure, ask me anything," I said.

"What's wrong with your mom?" he said.

"Oh, um, I don't know exactly," I told him the truth. I really didn't know exactly what was wrong, but I knew she was different than she used to be. "She has been different since my daddy died and she doesn't talk about it with me, but I try to help her take care of Kaylie and the house so she doesn't get too stressed out. We're kind of alone, ya' know."

"Jilly, you have plenty of people who care for you," Anton said.

"My mom, Kaylie, and now, a long-distance grandmother," I said.

"You have me, Jilly," Anton said, as he looked directly into my eyes and flashed his sweetest smile. My heart fluttered and I gulped. He set his bucket down and started collecting more broken glass. "You also have Aunt Lou and Uncle George, you know."

I smiled at him. Being around Anton made me feel happy, but not knowing what he was making with all that broken glass was *still* driving me nuts!

"What do you want with old, broken glass, Anton? When are you going to show me your project?" I asked. I just couldn't stand not knowing.

"The thing about broken glass, you see," he said, as he held up a pretty piece of red glass to the sunlight, "is that it may be broken, but it still sparkles when the sun hits it." Then he smiled again as he plopped the red glass into the bucket. Clearly, he wasn't ready to tell me yet.

"Ooh – look at this one," I said, as I held up a big, wavy piece of bright blue glass. "It reminds me of the ripples on the water, like the day we went to the river and I taught you how to skip a rock."

"That's definitely one for the bucket," he said, as he looked closer at the shiny blue glass and carefully placed it in the bucket.

We spent the rest of the day fixing up our old wagon, but it was pretty hopeless. We eventually gave up and went and jumped around the old tree trunks that were scattered alongside of the river. I wished that day could have lasted forever. As we walked home along the path to my house, he told silly jokes, one right after the other.

"What kind of water runs faster, hot or cold?" he asked.

"I don't know," I said.

"Hot, because everyone can catch cold!" he said, smiling.

By the time we got back, the sun was nearly set. The days were starting to get shorter now and he had to be home before dark, so he left right away. I sat by the rock garden and watched the evening sun set- ting in the distance. As the sun dipped lower, the few streaky clouds lit up in brilliant reds, yellows, oranges, and golds. I felt like it was a sign of how happy I was with mine and Anton's friendship. Our friendship was glorious, just like the sky.

Dear Sam,

I think Anton likes me! I am not sure, but he told me he cares 'bout me, which is a start, right? YES!

I think he is going to ask me to go to the dance with him. I am just sure of it. I can't believe I am going to go to my first school dance! Okay, I know he hasn't actually asked me yet, but I can feel it. I feel it in my bones, and in my stomach, but mostly, I feel it in my heart.

That's all for today. I don't want to talk about the bad because I just want to forget it.

Till next time,

 Jilly

THINK CRITICALLY...

- Jilly discovers that Brianna lied to Mr. Michael. How does this affect Jilly?
- How would you feel if this happened to you?

NOTES TO SELF:

CHAPTER FOURTEEN
Punch is Pink

The next day, it happened, I got asked to the dance! It didn't happen exactly the way I had hoped it would, but it happened, and that was enough for me. Anton's friend, Trina, invited me to the dance with her and a group of other girls and boys. Anton would be going with them. She said her mom could pick me up and drop me off, if I wanted to go. I knew Grams would want me to say yes, so I did. Besides, Grams wouldn't want me to let the dress go to waste.

In the days leading up to the dance, Trina and I started to hang out a little bit, mostly at lunch. She was really smart, but she was actually really nice, too. She was nothing like Brianna and her group of friends. I really started to feel like, maybe, I could belong here. Just maybe.

During study hall, I thought about how everything had moved so quickly for me since starting school here in September. October was just flying by like lightning. I couldn't wait!

It was Friday, and the big day was finally here. It was the day of the dance! When I saw Anton and Trina at lunch, all we could talk about was how excited we were for the dance that night. Mom had talked to Mr. Michael and gotten permission for me to attend the dance after all. Since it was unclear who copied who, he either needed to punish both of us or neither of us. So we both got to go to the dance, and I had to redo my paper.

Trina's mom was going to pick me up after school and I was going to get ready with her and the other girls. I was a mix of nervous and happy as I rode the bus home that night. Anton told me Aunt Lou was making him wear a suit and he promised his mom he would have a picture taken in it. I figured I should probably have one taken for Grams, too. She would want to see me all dressed up.

I was packing up all my stuff to go to Trina's when my mom yelled up to me that Trina was there. She had tears in her eyes as she hugged me really tight and told me to have fun, and to call her if I needed anything, *anything at all.* She said she knew Daddy was proud to be looking down on me tonight. I felt tears welling up in my eyes, but I kept 'em in.

At Trina's, we barely got ready in time because there were so many of us trying to get dressed in her tiny room. Her big sister did our make-up. Her dad took pictures of us all dressed up before we left, and her mom drove us in their very nice minivan. It was all very exciting!

I was sure the others could have heard my heart pounding if they hadn't been so loud on the way there. As we arrived at the dance, I felt like my heart was going to burst right out of my chest. I had to force myself to breath, and to calm down before we went in. I don't even know why we were laughing, but we couldn't stop.

As we walked through the door, I saw Anton. He was wearing a fine dark blue suit with a little flower on his suit jacket. He looked all grown up like that. I figured his mom was probably going to cry when she saw him, just like my mom did. He was very handsome all dressed up. I felt my cheeks get hot when he looked back at me and smiled.

Then I saw her. It was Brianna Maples. That little beast was standing right next to Anton, and as soon as she saw me, she marched right up to me with that hateful look on her face. I decided that no matter what, I was not going to let her get to me that night. Of course, I did not know how hard that was going to be.

"*Jillbilly,* what are you doing here? I thought Mr. Michael said you couldn't come to the dance, for stealing my work, *remember*?" she asked in her mean way. All of the look-alikes laughed when she spoke. It wasn't even funny.

"Stay away from me, Brianna, or I swear, I'll – just stay away," was all I said, and then I walked up to Anton and his friends, well, I guess, my friends, too. We all headed to the gymnasium floor that, for one night, had been transformed into a dance floor, with sparkly lights and all.

We stepped out on the dance floor and I don't know if we danced or laughed more, but it was fun. Then the slow song came on and everyone decided it was time to get some punch. As we stood around the refreshment table talking, Brianna and the look-alikes hovered nearby. They weren't dancing or anything.

I'm not sure why they were even there – they weren't having fun. Little did I know, they were planning a little fun of their own.

Anton and his friends were telling jokes when the DJ announced it was Lady's Choice – when the girls get to pick who they want to dance with. The song was good and fast, so Trina and the girls decided we should make the guys go out and dance with us. We each decided who we were going to take out on the dance floor, all at the same time. I chose Anton.

Just as I went for his arm, Brianna turned towards me with a full glass of bright pink punch, and one of her friends pretended to trip her. The pink splatter splashed across my face, and ran down the front of my pale blue dress like a waterfall on a mountainside. It even got on my sparkly silver shoes.

Brianna and her friends, who I just knew had planned this, stood there watching and laughing at me. They laughed right on cue, and so did everyone else. In the blink of an eye, it was all ruined, everything – the dress, the shoes, the dance, my night, and my entire life.

I turned and ran so fast that I slipped in the pool of punch and landed square on my butt in a bright pink puddle. I got up again, and walked very slowly, all the way out of the gym so as not to fall *again*. I could still hear them laughing as the doors closed behind me. I ran to the bleachers by the football field, and hid there. I cried so hard I thought I would run out of tears, but I didn't.

The breezy autumn night had started out like a

dream, but ended up being my worst nightmare. I heard Anton and Trina calling for me, but I couldn't look at them. I just sat there, in the dark, crying my eyes out. I could see the steam coming from my hot breath in the chilly air as I sat there alone under the stars. Yes, I was all alone.

I called Aunt Lou from my new cellphone and asked her to come and get me. She did, of course. She called Trina's mom and said she was driving me home from the dance. She tried to make me feel better, but there was no helping me at that point. The pain and embarrassment I felt after what Brianna did to me was the last straw. I was officially giving up on this place.

There was only one thing I looked forward to after that night: moving away. I would talk to Mom right away about getting moved out soon. The sooner the better!

The weekend after the dance, Anton tried and tried to reach me on my phone, but I did not answer. He even came to the house, but Mom told him I wasn't accepting visitors. I was so upset, I couldn't even tell Sam. I buried the pain, and the entire event, deep down inside. Maybe having friends just wasn't worth it.

On Monday, I went back to sitting by myself at lunch again and decided I would never talk to any of them again. Yes, that's right. I would go back to being alone. It was safer that way.

THINK CRITICALLY...

- Jilly starts out feeling one way in the beginning of this chapter, but feels very differently by the end. What happened and why do you think she feels so differently by the end of the chapter?

- Do you agree with Jilly's decision to leave the dance? Why or why not?

- Do you think that her treatment of her friends is fair?

- Why do you think she treats her friends differently after the dance?

NOTES TO SELF:

CHAPTER FOURTEEN

CHAPTER FIFTEEN
Friendships are like Rainbows

My plan worked pretty well, for a while. I ignored Anton and Trina, and all the other nice kids I had gotten to know. I just sat alone at lunch for the next few days. It was only another week until Thanksgiving break and then Anton would be going to Chicago to see his mom.

I felt a little bad because Trina and Anton had become pretty good friends of mine, but I just couldn't face anybody after the dance. Me and Mom and Kaylie would probably be moving on soon. I only had to wait a little while longer, and then I would never have to think about Blue Creek Middle School, or my first dance *fail*, again.

Every time I saw Brianna at school, she laughed and pretended like she was throwing her drink on me again, but it didn't bother me anymore. I actually felt kind of sorry for her. She was so pretty and she had so many nice things, but it was all just a cover up for how she was on the inside. I am guessing if I could see her heart, it would be all dark and rotten. I was just sure of it.

By the last day of school before Thanksgiving break, I was ready to get the day over with. Mom usually tried to move during school breaks, but no such luck. She said we were staying a while. If Mom wasn't ready to move on yet, this meant I would be going to school here after Thanksgiving break was over.

I decided I would just have to find a way to hide for the rest of the school year.

On the bus ride home on the last day before Thanksgiving break, Anton refused to let me ignore him any longer. He sat in my seat before I could sit down, so I chose another seat. He sat next to me in my new seat. Apparently, he was not giving up, so I let him sit there, but I turned my head towards the window and stared outside, pretending I was sitting alone.

I noticed it had started snowing. The first snow-fall of the year – usually, this was a happy time for me, but not now. I was still feeling pretty sorry for myself.

"Jilly, I know you're hurt and angry about what happened, but you can't let her win," Anton said. "You cannot give up on your friends like me and Trina, and everyone else who cares about you."

"Whatever," was all I could say, because I suddenly felt like if I talked, I would burst into tears.

I kept my head pointed towards the window so Anton couldn't tell I was about to cry. Watching the snow falling on the leaves made me feel a little better inside. Ignoring Anton did not stop him from talking to me, as I hoped it would.

"You can ignore me all you want, Jilly," he said. "Aunt Lou said I needed to give you time, and I did, but that time is up now. I refuse to let you feel sorry for yourself any longer. It stops right here, and right now."

I could feel the tears rising up over the lids of my eyes now. I don't know why I cried sometimes when people were trying to be nice to me when I felt bad. I refused to look at him, but he just kept going.

"I care about you, you – you're like my best friend, Jilly," he said, very seriously. "And I can't stand to see you like this. I tried to find you that night – we all did, Jilly. There are people at Blue Creek Middle School who really do care about you."

"And there are people who don't care about me," I said.

"I wouldn't go that far, but if you're talking about Brianna Maples, it doesn't matter where you go, there will always be mean, nasty people like her," he said. "They're everywhere, but they're outnumbered by the good people. You can't give up on your friends because of one bad person. That's not fair to us – and it's not fair to you, either!"

"I'm just a misfit here, like I was at every other school I've been too, Anton. I don't even know why you would want to be friends with me in the first place," I said.

"Because I'm a misfit, too, Jilly," he answered. "I don't even live with my own mom. I only get to see her a couple of times a year, and Trina, everyone treats her differently because she's in classes with kids who are older than her, and she's smarter than most of them, too. We're all misfits, Jilly, that's why we fit in so well together."

As the bus rolled to a stop at my house, he kept talking. "I'm leaving to go see my mom for Thanksgiving early in the morning, but I can't let things go like this."

I got off the bus, but that still didn't stop him. He yelled after me. "Meet me at the wagon at 4:30 today – *and don't be late!*"

As I walked the path to the old farmhouse, the tears fell harder. The winds picked up and made the tears feel cold against my face. I covered my neck with my scarf and walked faster. Mom was asleep when I went in. Kaylie was watching TV as usual. After turning off the TV, I made tomato soup for us for dinner and then I cleaned up the mess.

Mom was still sleeping. As the time got closer to 4:30, when I was supposed to meet Anton, I woke Mom up and asked if she could take care of Kaylie while I went to meet him. She said no, but I remembered how Grams *insisted* Mom go to dinner with her and it worked. I *insisted* that I get to go and see Anton one more time before he left for a visit with his mom. She eventually gave in. I got my winter boots on, and bundled up tight. Mom *insisted* I take a flashlight because it was getting dark earlier.

As I walked the snow-covered path towards the wagon, I remembered hunting with my daddy the last winter he was alive. I wondered if he was looking down at me now. Was he disappointed in me for not trying harder to fit in? I hoped not. Then I remembered how hard he tried not to fit in. That made me smile. He always had a way of making me feel better, even if he wasn't with me anymore.

As I approached the wagon, I could not believe what I saw. Anton was waiting there for me, all dressed up in his suit, with music playing on his phone. The wagon had been painted and decorated up. It was beautiful. I just couldn't believe my eyes.

"How did you do this?" I asked him, shocked at what I saw.

"After the leaves fell, I was able to find my way here from my house so you wouldn't know I was working on it," he said. "Plus, Trina helped. She said when we get back from Thanksgiving break, she wants to come out and hang out with us at the wagon – if it's okay with you."

"Of course, Anton, and I'm sorry if I hurt you," I told him. I was feeling really guilty on the inside for having ignored my friend for so long.

"Na, na, na," he said, in his special way. "I owe you a dance, Jilly," he said, as he took my hand and spun me around right there in the snow. As we danced, with the music playing in the background, and the snow falling all around us, I realized what having a true friend was all about. It was about caring for them during the good times and the bad times.

After the dance, he hugged me and told me I was his best friend, and that I had to promise to never let someone else come between our friendship again.

"I promise," I said.

Anton asked me to wait while he went in the wagon. He came out with a gift box.

"Uncle George helped me make it," he said, as he handed it to me. "Uncle George says that broken things sometimes make the most beautiful art – you just have to find a way to put the pieces back together again. Well, go ahead, open it."

I unwrapped it, and inside was the most beautiful piece of artwork I had ever seen. It was a metal frame in the shape of a tree. He used the metal from the dump to make the frame. All the leaves were made using the beautiful pieces of glass we found together. They had been washed and polished, and included all the colors of the rainbow, and then some.

"This is the art I was making, Jilly. It was for you. It has all the colors of our friendship inside of it," he said. "It's a tree because of the woods, but also because it's strong, like you, and like our friendship. Look – it even has the river, and this one here," he said, pointing at a yellow glass chunk on the tree. "It's for the school bus, where we first talked, and this little blue and white one is for the dress you wore to the dance."

"And what's this one for?" I asked, as I looked at a bright purple one embedded down into the tree trunk.

"That one was the one Kaylie found the day she disappeared and you and I worked together to find her," he said. "And this one here on the tree trunk, the little brown one, it's Mr. Squirrel – and these here, they're three baby pigs."

"Piglets," I said, as a smile snuck up on my face.

"Piglets," he said.

There were green chunks making up the grass, and brown pieces for the sand, there was even a bright yellow sun. I was speechless. By now the sun had dipped below the heavy snow clouds and a little ray of sunshine poked its head out. Anton took the stained glass tree from me and held it up to the light. As he did, it shone beautifully, like nothing I had ever seen before. Just as fast, the sunlight was gone, and the skies grew dark again.

I knew he had to leave. After we said our good-byes, he took off through the woods towards his house. I just sat there in the little wagon for a while, thinking about everything that happened since I came to Blue Creek Middle School. I picked up the lovely stained glass tree that Anton had made for me, and I saw something engraved on the back of the metal frame.

> *May the beauty within your heart, shine brighter than the broken parts.*
> *To my BFF, Jilly, the strongest and most beautiful girl at the dance. ~Anton*

When I turned the stained glass tree back over, I noticed a piece of heart-shaped glass right in the center of the tree. It was nestled deep within the tree's colorful leaves. I hung the stained glass tree on a branch near the entrance of the wagon. That way, every time I went there, I would be reminded of Anton's friendship.

I remembered all the fun times we had collecting broken pieces of glass just so he could turn them into something beautiful for me. This made me feel loved. He was a true friend like I ain't ever had before. I couldn't wait to see him, and Trina, again after Thanksgiving break.

Dear Sam,

I finally made a BFF. He's a boy, I always hoped for a girl BFF, but having a boy BFF is really just as good... even better. Things are going okay at Blue Creek Middle School, too. Mom says we are not going to be moving anytime soon. I guess that's okay.

Brianna is still quite beastly, but I realized that's who she is, and I can't do anything about it. I can only be me. If she doesn't like me for who I am, that's okay, too. I still have plenty of people who do like me just the way I am. I still have Anton, and Grams, and Trina, and of course, Mom, and Kaylie. Oh yeah, I have Aunt Lou and Uncle George, too.

I can't wait until Trina and Anton and I get to hang out at the wagon after Thanksgiving break!

Till next time,

 Jilly

THINK CRITICALLY...

- How does Jilly feel about her friendship with Anton at the end of this chapter?
- What changed between this chapter and the previous one to make Jilly feel different about their friendship?
- How can we tell we are in good, healthy friendships?

NOTES TO SELF:

EPILOGUE

It was Thanksgiving Day and some light snow had fallen on the ground. Anton was at his mom's for the holiday and everything was very quiet around our house. I had finally stopped feeling sorry for myself.

Grams called that morning. I told her all about everything that had happened since we last talked. I didn't tell her about Brianna because I didn't want her to know the pretty dress got ruined. Besides, Anton gave me the dance I missed, so everything was good now.

Mom and Kaylie were baking a pumpkin pie in the kitchen when Mr. Squirrel decided to pay us another visit. He was a lot smarter this time. After running along the counter, he jumped into the pantry and started squawking. It scared the daylights out of Kaylie, and Mom dropped the pie right in the middle of the floor. Mr. Squirrel squawked and chattered as Mom slammed the pantry door shut.

Mom called George to see if he could get the critter out of the pantry. He, of course, came right over. When George finished with the little critter, he asked if we would like to come down for Thanksgiving dinner. He said Lou had cooked as if Anton and the boys were still there and that if we didn't come, he'd have to eat it all by himself.

Mom agreed to go and we hopped in George's old work truck and headed down the old gravel road. George wasn't telling a fib, either. Aunt Lou cooked so much, I don't think I ever seen that much good food in one place, at one time, in my life! Lou even made a pumpkin pie, which was my favorite. We ate so much we thought our bellies might pop open. They didn't.

After Thanksgiving dinner, Mom laughed in the kitchen with Aunt Lou and Uncle George – that's what I decided to call them – they said it was okay. I taught Kaylie how to play video games, too. I imagined my daddy, *may he rest in peace*, was watching over us and smiling that day. I might not always fit in everywhere, but for now, I felt like I fit in just right, right where I was – with all the right people.

THINK CRITICALLY...

- How have Jilly's family and relationships changed since her first day at Blue Creek Middle School?
- What things do you think will happen with the characters after Thanksgiving Break? Jilly? Anton? Trina? Brianna? Jilly's Mom?

COMPARE WITH YOUR OWN EXPERIENCE...

- How are the characters in the book alike or different from your friends at school?
- What makes Jilly unique?
- Who do you relate to most in the story?
- How is Blue Creek Middle School alike or different from your school?
- What does bullying look like at your school?

USING SKILLS: SCENARIOS

Middle School can be tough, especially if you feel like a misfit. But using certain social skills could make it easier. The following pages highlight four key social skills that the characters in the story may have used at different times, which may have resulted in different outcomes. Think about the skill and the scenario, and how using the skill may have influenced the story.

INTRODUCING YOURSELF:

1. Look at the person. Smile.
2. Use a pleasant voice.
3. Offer a greeting. Say "Hi, my name is...."
4. Shake the person's hand.
5. When you leave, say "It was nice to meet you."

Jilly struggles initially because she doesn't know anyone and doesn't feel comfortable introducing herself. If she had used the skill of Introducing Yourself during the scenarios below, perhaps her experience would have been different. What do you think?

CHAPTER 1: Jilly describes how uncomfortable she is introducing herself in class.

> *"It wasn't the first sixth grade class I'd been to this year – and it probably wouldn't be the last, either. You would think I'd be good at introducing myself by now. Nope.*
>
> *I have been to at least 12 new schools since kindergarten. Every time I started a new school I had to get to know new kids, new teachers, and new rules. No matter how hard I tried, every school I went to, it seemed I didn't fit in. Oh well, here I go again."*

CHAPTER 3: Jilly sits alone on the bus.

> *"The bus wasn't the ideal place to reflect [on my day], but at least I didn't have to worry about anyone trying to interrupt me – nobody even talked to me that first day. As usual, I was totally alone and I felt like a complete misfit."*

CHAPTER 4: Jilly writes to Sam, her journal. She describes being alone at lunch, and wanting to skip it.

> *"Oh yeah, and I got in trouble AND no one sat with me at lunch. I wonder if I could just skip lunch until I get some friends. Hmmm. Something to think about."*

How could the skill of Introducing Yourself have helped Jilly in these scenarios?

DISAGREEING APPROPRIATELY:

1. Look at the person.
2. Use a pleasant voice.
3. Say "I understand how you feel."
4. Tell why you feel differently.
5. Give a reason.
6. Listen to the other person.

How might the story have been different if Jilly, Anton, or Brianna had used this skill of Disagreeing Appropriately during the scenarios below?

CHAPTER 1: Jilly is unhappy when Mrs. Jenkins wants to call her by her given name, Jillian.

"Oh, Ms. Jenkins?" I asked, in my most polite voice.

"Yes?" she said, just as polite as I did.

"Um, I have never gone by Jillian, so I would rather not start now if you don't mind," I said, with quite a lot of confidence. I added a nice smile to seal the deal. Whew, that was close.

"I do mind," she answered. "But the good news is you'll have a chance to become very comfortable hearing yourself called by your given name, Jillian."

She said it in such a way as to make it very clear there would be no more discussion on the topic. Some of the students giggled. Were they laughing at me? It was unacceptable. I had to act fast.

"Okay, Rose," I said, in exactly the same way she said my name.

CHAPTER 6: Jilly gets upset with Anton when Brianna acts condescendingly toward Anton and her, and then asks him to turn something in for her. Jilly feels like Anton is choosing Brianna over her.

"Why would you take that for her, Anton?" I asked. I couldn't believe he would be so nice to her.

"She's so – so – just mean. How could you do anything for that girl?"

"It's the polite thing to do, and you know that, Jilly," Anton said.

"No, I don't, and why did you tell her we were just having lunch?" I asked.

I didn't say more, but I felt betrayed by Anton. He was supposed to be my friend, not hers!

CHAPTER 7: Jilly and Brianna fight over roles when they are forced to be partners in a science lab.

As we worked on the frog dissection, she told me to do all the dissecting, while she did all the writing. When Mr. Johnson came by our table, he suggested we switch places. I took over the writing, and she took over the dissecting. She did not appreciate this. As soon as Mr. Johnson walked away, Brianna grabbed the pencil out of my hand and shoved the forceps towards me.

"No, Brianna, Mr. Johnson said we needed to switch," I said firmly, shoving the forceps back at her.

"I don't care what he said, I'm not dissecting this nasty little frog," she said, as she shoved the entire tray, frog and all, right back at me.

"Oh no – I am not getting in trouble because of you!" I said. The other students by us started looking our way. "You are just a spoiled little brat afraid to get your perfect little fingers dirty, and I'm not doing your work for you!"

"Oh yeah?" she said, with her voice really loud. "Well, you're just a silly little country girl who probably doesn't even know how to spell, so I'm not letting you do the writing!"

That's when it happened. She shoved the tray to me and I pushed back, and then all of a sudden, CRASH! Our tray, frog and all, hit the ground, and Mr. Johnson came walking over, with a not-so-happy look on his face.

All of this lands Jilly and Brianna on lunch detention until they can come to terms with each other.

For each of these scenarios, how might the story have gone differently if one or more of the characters was able to disagree appropriately? How might it have sounded (role-play to yourself or with a friend)?

ASKING FOR HELP:

1. Look at the person.
2. Ask the person if he or she has time to help you (now or later).
3. Clearly describe the problem or what kind of help you need.
4. Thank the person for helping you.

Jilly's family has moved around a lot, and they are used to not having too many people to count on. So there are times when those in the family may not be comfortable—or may not know how—to Ask for Help. Think about the scenarios below, and imagine how the events could have been different had someone asked for help.

CHAPTER 5: Jilly comes home and finds her sister, Kaylie, missing. Her mom had fallen asleep and Kaylie had wandered off. This is the second time since the story started that Kaylie had been left unsupervised due to Jilly's mom's illness and exhaustion. (Earlier, Kaylie walks in with stew boiling over on the stove.)

What if Jilly's mom had been able to ask for help earlier on? What if Jilly had felt comfortable speaking to a trusted adult about the trouble her mom was having, and that she needed help?

CHAPTER 10: Jilly goes to hang out with Anton, and comes home to find Kaylie crying and her mother on the kitchen floor, having hurt herself. Jilly is able to run and get help from Anton's family, and take her mom to the hospital. But had she not come home when she did, and had she not known Anton's family, things could have been much different – especially since the family didn't have a telephone to call for help.

What steps does Jilly's family take after this event to make sure there is a support system in place to help them if they need it?

CHAPTERS 13–14: Throughout the book, Jilly is teased, and then bullied by Brianna and her friends. Things escalate when Brianna accuses Jilly of cheating, and then she and her friends spill punch on Jilly at the dance, ruining her dress. Jilly reacts by running away and hiding from embarrassment. She avoids her friends, and just wants to be left alone.

Jilly had asked Brianna to stop at various times in the story, but she did not stop. What if Jilly had been able to ask a trusted adult for help handling the pervasive situation?

MAKING AN APOLOGY:

1. Look at the person.
2. Use a serious, sincere voice tone, but don't pout.
3. Begin by saying "I wanted to apologize for..." or "I'm sorry for...."
4. Do not make excuses or try to rationalize your behavior.
5. Sincerely say you will try not to repeat the same behavior in the future.
6. Offer to compensate or pay restitution.
7. Thank the other person for listening.

Knowing how to apologize to someone when you are wrong is an important skill to have. It takes a lot of courage. This is especially true when you feel like the other person should be apologizing to you as well. But it doesn't always work out that way. You can't control the behavior of others, only your own behavior.

How might the scenarios below have gone differently if the characters had apologized to one another in an appropriate, timely way?

CHAPTER 1: Jilly responds out of anger and embarrassment to Mrs. Jenkins when she refuses to call Jilly by her preferred name. The result is that Jilly has to write an apology to Mrs. Jenkins, which is time-consuming, and gets their relationship off to a rough start.

What if Jilly had apologized to Mrs. Jenkins after class, and then used the skill of Disagreeing Appropriately to calmly explain her name preference? Would things have gone differently?

CHAPTERS 6-9: Jilly struggles with when and how to apologize to Anton. She knows she wants to, but doesn't have the skills to do it, so she keeps dragging on the discomfort and disagreement. She finally gets the strength to apologize in Chapter 9.

>*"Can I just talk to you outside for a minute? It'll just be a minute, I swear," I said. I don't know why, but it felt like my heart was beating faster.*
>
>*"What?" he said as he walked out onto the porch.*
>
>*"I'm sorry. I really acted like a, um, a..."*
>
>*"Na, na, na – Jilly, don't say anything. I should not have let her treat you like that. I should be the one to say I'm sorry, so, I'm sorry," he said, and made a kind of half smile.*
>
>*"No, Anton, I acted like, like my sister Kaylie when she doesn't get her way. I understand what you were saying. Brianna was wrong – not you," I said. There, it was over, at last!*

What if Jilly had apologized to Anton on the way home, or right away? Or what if Anton had calmly approached Jilly and asked her to talk?

FINAL THOUGHTS:

- What other social skills do you think characters in the story would benefit from learning and using?
- What do you think is next for Jilly and her family and friends?

Boys Town Press Featured Titles
Kid-friendly books to teach social skills

978-1-934490-94-5

978-1-944882-03-7

978-1-944882-10-5

978-1-944882-21-1

978-1-944882-32-7

978-1-934490-66-2

978-1-934490-79-2

978-1-944882-06-8

978-1-934490-66-2

More books from the Boys Town Press

978-1-934490-54-9

978-1-934490-60-0

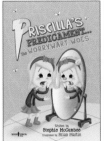

978-1-934490-87-7

978-1-934490-77-8

For Young Readers

978-1-944882-24-2

978-1-944882-29-7

978-1-944882-18-1

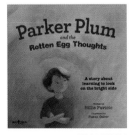

978-1-944882-33-4

BoysTownPress.org

For information on Boys Town, its Education Model®, Common Sense Parenting®, and training programs:
boystowntraining.org , boystown.org/parenting
EMAIL: training@BoysTown.org, PHONE: 1-800-545-5771

For parenting and educational books and other resources:
BoysTownPress.org, EMAIL: btpress@BoysTown.org, PHONE: 1-800-282-6657